D0951915

Once
in a
Lifetime

Once in a Lifetime

MARY MONROE

www.kensingtonbooks.com

DAFINA BOOKS are published by

Kensington Publishing Corp.
119 West 40th Street
New York, NY 10018

All Kensington titles, imprints, and distributed lines are available at special quantity discounts for bulk purchases for sales promotion, premiums, fund-raising, educational, or institutional use. Special book excerpts or customized printings can also be created to fit specific needs. For details, write or phone the office of the Kensington Special Sales Manager: Attn. Special Sales Department. Kensington Publishing Corp., 119 West 40th Street, New York, NY 10018. Phone: 1-800-221-2647.

The DAFINA logo is a trademark of Kensington Publishing Corp.

Library of Congress Card Catalogue Number: 2021936519

ISBN-13: 978-1-4967-3063-3
ISBN-10: 1-4967-3063-1
First Kensington Hardcover Edition: October 2021

ISBN-13: 978-1-4967-3064-0 (e-book)
ISBN-10: 1-4967-3064-X (e-book)

10 9 8 7 6 5 4 3 2 1

Printed in the United States of America

This book is dedicated to these amazing queens: Mitzi Dunn, Ella Curry, Gwen Richardson, Dr. Maxine Thompson, Tara Worthy, Meredith Riley, Cynthia Simmons, Lauretta Pierce, Pam Nelson, Sheila Sims, and Maria Felice Sanchez.

ACKNOWLEDGMENTS

It is such an honor to be a member of the Kensington Books family.

Esi Sogah is an amazing editor! I'd be lost without her. Thank you, Esi, for helping turn my "ugly ducklings" into swans. Thanks to Steven Zacharius, Adam Zacharius, Vida Engstrand, Lauren Jernigan, Michelle Addo, Norma Perez-Hernandez, Stephanie Finnegan, Robin E. Cook, Susie Russenberger, Darla Freeman, the wonderful crew in the sales department, and everyone else at Kensington for working so hard for me.

Thanks to the fabulous book clubs, bookstores, libraries, my readers, and the magazine and radio interviewers for supporting me for so many years.

To my incredible literary agent, Andrew Stuart, thank you for always looking out for me.

Please continue to e-mail me at Authorauthor5409 @aol.com and visit my website at www.Marymonroe. org. You can also communicate with me on Facebook at Facebook.com/MaryMonroe and Twitter@Mary MonroeBooks.

Peace and blessings,

Mary Monroe

Once
in a
Lifetime

CHAPTER 1

November 1, 2014

I never would have guessed that an encounter with two strangers would change my life forever. Even if I had known in advance what fate had in store for me, I would not have changed a thing.

There was nothing extraordinary about my life. At the age of thirty-two, I had settled into a comfortable routine. I had a lot to be thankful for: a good education, a great job, excellent health, a nice apartment in a San Jose, California, suburb, and a family and friends I adored. I managed my money well, so I lived a fairly comfortable lifestyle, which included frequent out-of-town vacations each year.

I had a very short bucket list by now: marriage, children, and a nice house. But after I turned thirty, people stopped asking me when I was going to get married. Everybody knew I was impulsive and strong

minded and insisted that it turned off a lot of men—
especially the ones I kept getting involved with. Still
being single didn't bother me. I wasn't quite ready to
give up my freedom anyway. I wanted to do more
things on my own terms. Especially more traveling.
Having a husband would mean we'd have to agree on
how much money to spend, where to go, when, and
what to do once we got there. On some of my previous adventures, there had been times when I'd only
wanted to spend the day kicking back on the beaches
or stretched out in my hotel bed watching TV.

I'd already visited some of the most intriguing
cities in the world, but one of the places I still wanted
to see was Paris, France. I thought about it a lot. And
so did Mama and Daddy.

I had been with them for about an hour that Saturday morning. We had discussed some of the same
subjects we discussed on a regular basis, and a few
new ones. One was my plan to spend the week of
Christmas in Paris this year. My parents rarely inter-
fered in my personal life. And when they did, I took it
in stride. They knew by now that no matter what
they said, I was going to do whatever I wanted.

"I don't like the idea of you going way over there
by yourself," Daddy told me in a concerned tone.
"I thought Madeline and Odette were going to go
with you."

"I thought the same thing. I've been waiting for

them for almost ten years," I replied. "I'd like to go while I'm still fairly young, so I've decided to go alone."

"There's a lot of criminal activity going on in Europe," Daddy continued.

"Aw, hush up, Alex. There's a lot of criminal activity going on over here, too," Mama scolded as she wagged her finger in Daddy's face. She turned to me with a smile. "Baby, as long as you're careful, you'll enjoy Paris as much as I did. Before you leave, make sure you pack everything you'll need. Especially your passport."

"I couldn't find it."

Mama gave me a stern look and shook her head. "Vanessa, as much as you like to travel, you of all people should keep your passport in a safe place at all times."

"It was in a safe place. I think I accidentally threw it out the last time I purged my files. But I applied for a new one last month. The clerk said I should receive it in three or four weeks." I paused and scratched the side of my neck and gave Mama a thoughtful look. "The funny thing is, it's been that long already. Oh well. I'm sure it'll arrive any day. That's the least of my worries right now. I'm hungry! Let's go out to dinner this evening. My treat. What'll it be this time—Chinese, Mexican, or Italian?" I sprang up from the easy chair facing Mama and Daddy on the floral couch in the suite they resided in at the Alliance Retirement Home.

"Honey, we'd love to eat out with you again. We've already made plans for this evening, though." Mama swallowed hard and gave me a sympathetic look. "Vanessa, we appreciate all you do for us. But you need to focus more on yourself. You don't have to spend so many of your Saturday nights with us like you've been doing."

"I love coming over here to visit and chat," I protested.

"You mean to 'check up' on us," Daddy teased. He snorted and gave me a stern look. "This place has more orderlies and nurses than you can shake a stick at. That was one of the main reasons we chose this particular facility. Moving here was the best decision we ever made. Don't worry about us."

My parents were both approaching seventy and still in fairly good shape. They ate healthy meals, only consumed alcohol every now and then, and got a decent amount of exercise. Daddy had a weakness for sweets, so he was about twenty pounds overweight, and all of his hair was gray. But he was still one of the most attractive senior citizens I knew. I had inherited his round face, big brown eyes, and reddish-brown complexion. Mama, also slightly overweight but still attractive, had arthritis in one of her knees and occasionally had to use a walker. But nothing slowed them down when they wanted to do something. Their lives were as active as mine. I still worried about them, though.

I took a deep breath and continued, speaking in a slightly firmer tone. "Daddy, you told me that some of the residents here are bored, lonely, and depressed because their family members rarely visit them."

"Pffftt!" Mama gave me a dismissive wave. "We never have time to be bored, depressed, or lonely. Your brother was here again yesterday evening and didn't know when to leave. He made us late for our shuffleboard game."

"My godson and his wife stopped by and took us to Red Lobster, day before yesterday. Your sister and her husband came three days in a row last week," Daddy said.

"We put too much responsibility on you when you were still in school. Your time is all yours now. Live the life you deserve before it's too late," Mama added.

I hated when my parents talked like this. I loved them and would have done anything in the world to make them comfortable in their old age. I'd even helped them pick out the retirement home. It was plain looking and on a dead-end street. But it was safe and well kept. My baby sister, Debra, compared it to that gloomy motel featured in the movie *Psycho*, but our brother, Gary, thought it was a great choice.

It was only two blocks from our church and other conveniences. Daddy still owned the Buick he'd been driving for five years, but they usually called Uber when he didn't feel like driving. And whenever they wanted me to drive them somewhere, I never hesitated. Debra and Gary helped out as much as they would let them, but I was always the first one they called. One of the reasons was because my twenty-two-year-old sister had two-year-old twin sons and they kept her busy. Gary, who was twenty-five, worked as a welder for a company in Oakland. He drove fifty miles each way, five days a week, so his days were very long. He also spent a lot of time with his girlfriend, so it wasn't easy for him to visit Mama and Daddy. I had a busy life, too. But because I was the eldest and had more time to spare, I felt it was my obligation to be available to assist my parents as much as possible.

Unlike some of the dozens of other residents at the home who occupied small, no frills rooms, my parents had a spacious suite. It was large enough to accommodate two full-size beds, a couch, a few other living room items, and they had a patio with lounge chairs. After maintaining our four-bedroom family home for over thirty-five years, they'd decided that they wanted to live the rest of their years more simply. I'd tried to talk them into selling the house and buying a small condo. That hadn't interested them at all. They'd laughed when I invited them to move into my two-bedroom, one-bath apartment with me.

"I am living the life I deserve," I insisted.

"What happened to Barry?" Daddy asked with one eyebrow raised. "You haven't mentioned him since he had dinner with us last month."

"Oh. Well, things didn't work out with him," I admitted. "But we're still going to be friends, though." I didn't want to tell my folks that Barry Lockett had given me an ultimatum: accompany him to Maine where he'd been offered a position at the high school he had attended, or he'd go without me. Even though he'd previously implied that we'd eventually get married, I'd declined his offer. As much as I had cared about him, he was a little too controlling and irresponsible, so I was not about to quit my dream job and uproot myself for him. Three days after he'd had dinner with my parents, two weeks before Halloween, he sent me an e-mail in the middle of the night to let me know that he was ending our relationship. To add insult to injury, he also told me in the e-mail not to contact him because he didn't want to hear anything I had to say. I checked his Facebook page last week to see what he was up to. Even though his new job wouldn't start until September, I was surprised to discover that he had already moved to Maine.

"That's a shame. It would have been nice to have a

schoolteacher in the family. Well, you're still fairly young and you look good. There is plenty of time to figure out your future. But don't squander your time, sugar. Buh-leeve me, life goes by faster than folks realize," Mama said. She gave me another sympathetic look, something she did quite often. "Why don't you go visit your sister this evening? I'd hate for you to be over there in that apartment by yourself. Debra's still trying to get the house fixed up to her liking and maybe you can help."

My sister and her husband had eagerly accepted our parents' invitation to move into the house we'd been raised in after Mama and Daddy moved to the retirement home four months ago. They had paid off the mortgage, so Debra and Stephen only had to pay for maintenance, property taxes, and homeowners' fees. I rolled my eyes. "I'll pass on that. They have out-of-town company this weekend *again*," I replied.

"What about Madeline and Odette? You three have been joined at the hips for years," Daddy tossed in.

"I'm having coffee with them after church tomorrow. Anyway, they usually spend their Saturday evenings doing things with their families. I'm glad I'm still free to do whatever I want," I muttered with a mild sigh.

Mama had worked as a flight attendant for more than thirty-five years. She'd spent days at a time away from home in fabulous places like Rome, London,

Tokyo, and Paris. Daddy had managed a night shift crew for a meatpacking company even longer. I'd spent some of my best high school and college years supervising Debra and Gary and taking care of the house. Even though I was glad to do it, I'd promised myself that when they got old enough to take care of themselves, I'd make up for all the parties and other good times I hadn't been able to enjoy with my friends. Daddy had helped when he could, and he'd occasionally hired a woman to do some of the cooking and cleaning. So, I had never complained.

A month after Gary finished high school, he joined the navy. After his discharge three years later, he enrolled in a welding school and moved into an apartment with two of his friends. Six months after Debra received her high school diploma, she chose to marry her long-term boyfriend instead of going to college. She promised Mama and Daddy that she would resume her education later and that appeased them. I was happy for Debra, and even happier that my "babysitting" responsibilities had finally come to an end.

A week after Debra's wedding, I hopped on a plane to Puerto Vallarta, Mexico, and spent ten days. The following year, I enjoyed a week in Hawaii. I took weekend jaunts to Vegas and Reno several times a year, and when I turned thirty, I treated myself to a weeklong cruise to the Bahamas. I was so impulsive I couldn't sustain a relationship with a man for more than a few months. That was fine by me. But the men I dated couldn't deal with that.

A lot of people, including my family, had begun to predict that because of my devil-may-care attitude, no man would ever marry me. I was not about to change my ways just to land a husband, or even a serious boyfriend. Being who I was meant a lot to me, even if it meant I'd grow old alone.

CHAPTER 2

My two best friends, Madeline Lilly and Odette Wheeler, had decided to marry their boyfriends while they were still in college. Before they'd started having babies and tending to their husbands, we spent as much time as possible together. Madeline's family used to live next door to mine, so she and I had been friends since we were in elementary school. We'd hooked up with Odette at South Bay City High at the same table during lunchtime in the cafeteria. Madeline and I were the same age and Odette was three years older, but that didn't stop us from becoming close. We'd even been in a few of the same classes. I'd had a lot of other friends over the years, but these two were almost as close to me as my sister.

We'd started making plans to spend a Christmas in Paris shortly after I turned twenty-two. But each time we got close to finalizing our plans, something more important came up with one or both of them. We didn't go last year because Madeline had to have emergency dental surgery the month before our departure. The year before that, Odette's husband had an automobile accident and had to spend every day from November until the end of December in the hospital.

Madeline and Odette had accompanied me to Vegas and a few other places, but traveling was not as important to them. The times I had traveled alone or with a tour group of strangers, I'd had fun anyway. I would have already visited Paris, but since Madeline and Odette were interested in going, I'd put it off because of them. But now I had run out of patience and I wasn't going to put it off any longer.

After I'd graduated from our community college ten years ago with a degree in business administration, I worked as a temp at several companies for the following year. I prayed for a position that I could really sink my teeth into. The next year, I accepted a permanent position at South Bay City Construction. Within a month, I knew I was in the right place. It was a small but very successful family-owned company located in the financial district of our city. The pay was reasonable, the benefits were fantastic, and I worked with some wonderful people. This was where I planned to stay until I retired.

In the meantime, I was going to continue enjoying

life. I had been looking forward to my upcoming vacation for months.

When two more weeks went by and I still had not received my passport, I became very concerned. One of the things I was worried about was the fact that if I didn't cancel my plans twenty-one business days before the departure date, I couldn't get a refund. I had almost reached that deadline, so I had to do it by this coming Thursday. I counted every penny I earned, so I didn't like to lose any money if I didn't have to. But it was the week before Thanksgiving now—five weeks since I'd applied for a new passport—and I still hadn't received it. I was getting worried, so I finally called the passport office on Monday to follow up. "Ma'am, your passport was mailed out a week and a half ago."

I was stunned. "W-what? Are you sure?" I asked.

"That's what my records indicate," the woman replied in a stiff tone.

"Could you verify the mailing address, please?" I didn't give her time to respond. I rattled off my address as clearly as possible.

"That's the address I have, ma'am."

"Well, my passport never arrived. I'd like to reapply. I need to have it by December twentieth. That's the day I leave for Paris."

"You're welcome to reapply. But this time of year,

it could take anywhere from four to eight weeks to process the replacement."

"I'll pay extra to have it expedited."

"You're welcome to do that. However, it would still take anywhere from three to four weeks, maybe even longer. I'm so sorry. Would it be possible for you to reschedule your travel plans?" The woman sounded sincerely sympathetic, but that didn't make me feel any better.

It felt like somebody had let the air out of me. "I guess I'll have to. Thank you," I muttered.

I didn't like making personal calls from work. Especially to a government office where you could be put on hold for a very long time. During the thirty-three minutes I had to wait for someone to help me today, one of our construction team members approached me with a few requests. After he left, Dennis McNabb, the fifty-year-old office busybody, shuffled past my desk three times in ten minutes with an amused look on his pudgy face, which usually meant he had some juicy gossip to share. Anna Wong, one of the bookkeepers and my closest friend at work, had stopped by two minutes ago and dropped off a cup of coffee and a bagel for me. "Call me," she mouthed before skittering back to her workstation, three doors down the hall from mine. I didn't have my own office or occupy a cubicle. But my desk was located in front of my boss's office. It faced a huge window, so I had a great view of downtown.

After I hung up the telephone, and before I could take the first sip of my coffee, Dennis returned. "Guess who I stumbled into the other night," he began. His gossip was more amusing than malicious, so I didn't mind listening to him regale me with mundane comments about how he'd seen one of the guys in the mail room having dinner Saturday night with one of our married secretaries. "They looked pretty cozy to me, if you know what I mean." When I told Dennis that the secretary and the mail room guy were cousins, he chuckled, lost interest in the story, and scurried back to his cubicle at the end of the hall.

Before I could call Anna, Jim Leafe, our executive manager, strode out of his office and stopped by the side of my desk. "Vanessa, how are you coming along with the Reynolds report?" One of the many things I liked about my company was that we were all on a first-name basis. I had such a good relationship with Jim, I didn't mind when he asked me to do things that were not related to my job. This morning before I could even turn on my computer, he'd rushed out of his office on the way to his first meeting and given me the keys to his Lexus. "Drop it off at my mechanic's shop in the next hour. They're expecting you." I never balked or refused when Jim asked me to do personal things for him because he always compensated me with flowers, expensive lunches, or a few hours off with pay. Everybody I knew said I had the best boss in the world, and I agreed.

"It's in your in-box, sir," I chirped with my chest puffed out. I worked hard at being efficient and it paid off. Each year I received generous pay increases and bonuses. "I finished it an hour ago."

Jim glanced at his watch. "Hmmm. What about the Williams project?"

"It's also in your in-box."

He gave me a huge smile and a thumbs-up. "Excellent! As usual, I knew I could count on you!" Jim was extremely fit for a man in his late fifties with four grown children and eight grandchildren. And it was no wonder. He played racquetball on a regular basis with members of the country club he belonged to, and he ran three miles, five times a week. Even with his bright green eyes and thick silver hair, he was not classically handsome. But you would have thought he looked like a movie star by the confident way he carried himself. Before he turned away, he said, "Young lady, if you ever leave this company, I'm going to go with you." We laughed.

CHAPTER 3

There was more than one reason I was almost obsessed with spending a Christmas in Paris. When I'd first started thinking about being a world traveler in middle school, it was one of the many top cities already on my long list. Mama had sharpened my interest. She had told me about the wonderful times she'd had there with Daddy, and on her own. "Of all the cities I've been to, Paris is the most magical one. Each time I was there I felt like a new and better woman, especially if it was during Christmastime," she had told me. "And they treat black folks better than any city I've ever visited." That was when I decided it would be my most important future trip, and it had to be on or near Christmas Day. After waiting so long and getting so close, I was very disappointed that it wouldn't be this year.

I called Anna's extension twenty minutes before

noon and got her voice mail. "I can't do lunch today. I have a personal matter I need to take care of. I'll give you all the details later." I decided to cancel my vacation today instead of waiting until Thursday. The sooner I got it over with, the better I'd feel. And I wouldn't make any more travel plans until I had my passport in my hand.

The travel agency where I'd been booking my vacations for the past eight years was located on the ground floor of a small, redbrick building two blocks from my office on the same street. When I got there at five minutes past twelve, Sharon Salas, the same buxom, middle-age blonde who had made most of my arrangements over the years, rose from her seat at the desk closest to the entrance as soon as she saw me. The three other agents, who all reported to Sharon, were busy assisting other clients. They all waved and smiled as soon as they spotted me. Each time I visited, flashy new posters of exotic locations had replaced the previous ones on each wall and in the front windows. Large live plants, flyers, and brochures were displayed all over the place. "Hello, Vanessa! Good to see you again!" Sharon exclaimed with a wide smile on her cute, rosy-cheeked face. She motioned for me to take the chair next to her desk. I was too antsy to sit, so I stood in front of her, shifting my weight from one foot to the other. "You must be counting the days to takeoff. Boy, do I envy you."

"Sharon, I have a problem," I blurted out. Her demeanor changed immediately. There was a stiff look on her face now.

"Nothing too serious, I hope," she said, blinking rapidly. "I know how important this trip is to you."

"It still is. But my passport has been delayed and I don't know when it'll arrive." I let out a loud breath and flopped down in the chair anyway.

"Oh! So, you've come to reschedule?" Sharon opened one of her drawers and pulled out a manila folder with my name in big bold black letters on the tab. "No problem at all. Let's see what we can do and—"

I held up my hand and shook my head. "No. The whole idea was to spend the week of Christmas in Paris this year."

Sharon set my file down and gave me a serious look. "I can assure you that Paris is an excellent choice for a vacation any time of the year. I always go in the springtime. There is nothing like a slow cruise down the Seine River and a visit to the Louvre to lift a person's spirits."

"I know," I said in a tired tone. "I was really looking forward to doing that and a lot more. I'm going to apply for a replacement passport, but I doubt if it'll arrive in time."

"I see. Does this mean you want to cancel?"

"I don't have a choice. I've paid for my trip in full and I can't risk losing that much money. So, I'm going to need to cancel for now."

"I'm so sorry to hear that. When you're ready to rebook, just let me know. Now if you'll follow me to Peggy's office, she'll do the paperwork and issue you a refund check." I dragged my feet as I followed Sharon down a short hall that also had posters covering the walls. Fifteen minutes later, I was on my way back to the office with my refund check. I still had most of my lunch hour left so I went across the street to my bank and deposited the check.

When I got back to the office, Anna was sitting in the visitor's chair by the side of my desk. "Well?" she said, with her arms folded and a puzzled look on her cute face. With her long black hair in a ponytail and the casual attire Jim encouraged us to wear, she looked more like a teenager than a woman of twenty-eight. She'd been with the company for four years. "What's the big mystery?" she asked, smoothing down the sides of her skinny jeans.

I told her about my missing passport and having to cancel my trip. Even though Anna was younger than me, she was very mature and often gave great advice.

She was the only person I knew who liked to travel as much as I did. She and her family had spent their frequent vacations visiting cities in every continent on the planet. Both of her parents still had relatives in China, so they went there at least once every two years. Her father was a software executive at a company with offices in San Francisco, LA, and Hong Kong.

Anna had accompanied me to Hawaii and Mexico twice. Unfortunately, her husband of two years was not only a homebody—he had a fear of flying. So she had slowed down considerably. She had already visited Paris four times and had become bored with it, so I couldn't talk her into going with me. Besides, she was way more interested in trying to conceive her first child, which she'd been trying to do since she got married.

"Well, since you won't be visiting the City of Lights, how would you like to go with Gus and me to spend Christmas in Maui?" Anna rolled her eyes and added, "His brother bought a new house there a year ago and Gus has finally agreed to go."

"Thanks for asking, and it's really tempting. But I'll take a rain check. I really had my heart set on Paris," I replied, unable to keep a whiny tone out of my voice.

Mama was the next person I told that I'd canceled

my travel plans. I called her up when I got home from work Monday evening. "Baby, I'm so sorry you won't be able to go on your trip. I know how much you were looking forward to it," she told me in a soothing tone. I asked her not to mention what I'd just told her to Daddy or my siblings until I told them, which I was not ready to do yet. Even though I knew that they would feel sorry for me and try to make me feel better, I wasn't ready to be pitied. "When you do get your passport, make plans for next Christmas, unless you want to go some other time during the year."

"I might do that, Mama. Oh well. What are you and Daddy doing for dinner? I don't feel like cooking," I mumbled.

"We're going to the movies this evening and tomorrow we're going to drive down to Carmel with the Kesslers to spend a few days. They recently bought a timeshare near the beach. We'll be back on Friday."

"That's good. I'm so glad you and Daddy are keeping yourselves busy. So many elderly people get sedentary too soon."

"Pffftt. We didn't retire so we could sit around and turn to mush. My sister Pauline is two years younger than me and she's so inactive her doctor keeps warning her that she is going to develop osteoporosis if she doesn't get more exercise. Her husband's already got it. That's why they haven't left New Jersey for the past three years," Mama said. "Oh, before I forget. Your sister came by earlier today. She said she's going to give you a call this evening. That Debra. Something tells me she wants you to babysit again this weekend."

"I'll call her," I said in a tired tone. I loved my baby sister to death, and I enjoyed spending time with her and her family. I babysat her children at least three or four times a month. On top of providing free child-care services to my sister (and other relatives and friends), I came through for Debra when she needed a loan. And so did a few other relatives and friends. I was the go-to girl for so many things. Gary had recently hit me up for five hundred dollars, so he could get some work done on his car. Before that, he'd talked me into going on a few dates with his girl-friend's divorced brother because he was depressed and that was depressing everybody in the family. Unfortunately, before I could develop a relationship with the brother, he reconciled with his wife.

Even though Mama had been warning me all my life that being too accommodating could encourage people to take advantage of my kindness, I enjoyed pleasing people. I knew she was right, and I turned down requests every now and then. But at the end of the day, I usually ended up doing another favor for whomever I'd said no to.

Another thing Mama told me over and over was that one day I would be "rewarded" for all my good deeds. I hoped that day wasn't too far away. I couldn't think of anybody who deserved some compensation as much as I did.

CHAPTER 4

After work on Wednesday, Anna and I had dinner at Olive Garden. Afterward, we returned to the office to work out in the small company fitness center located right next to our break room. I was ready to throw in the towel after only forty minutes, but Anna decided to stay another thirty minutes. "If you hadn't let me eat all that bread, I wouldn't need to stay here so long," she complained, huffing and puffing as she trotted on one of the three treadmills. The only other equipment were two stationary bikes and some weights, which we rarely touched.

"I ate just as much as you," I reminded as I stuffed my towel into my backpack.

"Yeah, but if I were five feet six like you and not five feet one, I wouldn't have to worry about it because there'd be more places for the fat to settle. Besides, if I lose at least five pounds by next week, I can really enjoy that Thanksgiving feast you're cooking.

That's all Gus has been talking about since I told him." Anna stopped and gave me a sympathetic look. "Too bad Barry won't be around to join us."

I shrugged. "I'm sure we'll have a great time without him anyway."

Despite the fact that I had cared a lot about Barry, I had almost put him out of my mind. The only time I thought about him now was when somebody else brought up his name.

"Since we're already on the subject, when are you going to start dating again?" Anna wanted to know.

"When I meet somebody interesting."

Debra dropped by my office Thursday afternoon, a few minutes after two p.m. She and Gary had Mama's smooth chocolate skin; curly, jet-black hair; and keen features. As usual, she was dressed to the nines in a light blue jumpsuit with a matching jacket and shiny black leather boots. Gary and I worked out regularly, so weight had never been a big issue with us. But Debra loved sweets even more than Daddy, so she was always trying to lose weight. Every year since she was a teenager, she'd lost twenty pounds in about six months and gain it all back six months later.

We had been spoiling her from the day she was born. Now her husband of four years was doing it as well. Stephen was a reporter for our local newspaper and didn't make much money. But his parents owned a body shop and he and Debra never hesitated to go to them (and me) when they needed a loan.

"My dentist just moved his office across the street from here," Debra began. "My cleaning didn't take as long as I thought it would. I was at loose ends, so I decided to come over and say hello to you." She snorted and gave me a curious look. "Stephen and I stopped by your apartment last night and you weren't home."

"Anna and I treated ourselves to dinner and then we came back here to work out," I replied. "Are you and Stephen still spending Thanksgiving with his family? If not, I'll have plenty of food if you all want to come over."

"I wish we could. But we can't disappoint his folks. They are really looking forward to seeing the kids again. By the way, are you still going to Paris for Christmas?"

I drew in a deep breath and the last words I wanted to say rolled off my tongue like pebbles. "I had to cancel. My passport got lost in the mail."

I didn't like the hopeful look on Debra's face. "Really? That's a shame." She cleared her throat. "Remember that Christmas Eve party I told you Stephen was cohosting with his friend Roger?"

"I remember. Is it still on?"

"Yup!"

"Well, what about it?"

"It's going to be held at Roger's apartment and we're having trouble finding somebody to keep the kids for us. Mama and Daddy are going on that holiday cruise to Mexico that the retirement center organized. Stephen's parents have to attend a church event and all of my friends have plans for that night. Do you think either Madeline or Odette would babysit for us?"

My mouth dropped open and I looked at Debra like she was crazy. "Seriously? You know how busy my friends are. Madeline and her family are spending Christmas in Berkeley with Kirk's family. And several of Odette's out-of-town folks will be staying at her house that night. I'm sure it's too late to book a flight to Reno for that week, so I'll probably drive up there. Harrah's offered me a free room for four nights and the offer expires two days after Christmas."

Debra let out a deep sigh and gave me a woeful look. "Oh well. If you change your mind about going to Reno, the kids can stay with you. Otherwise, we'll have to hire a professional sitter to come spend the night. It'll cost us a pretty penny, though. And, as you know, I spent more than I should have getting the house repainted and a few new pieces of furniture. Stephen won't get another raise until February. We've already borrowed from his folks this month. And, I don't like borrowing from Mama and Daddy too often. Gary's always broke, so I can't hit him up for a loan, and—"

I interrupted my long-winded sister by holding up my hand. Instead of advising her on how she and Stephen should manage their money better, I said, "How much do you want to borrow from me this time?"

"Well, I'll need enough to pay an all-night sitter, and a few extra dollars to have on hand in case I go over my gift budget. How much have you got?"

I loved Debra, but she could be very exasperating. "Stop beating around the bush and give me a number," I prodded.

She gave me a hopeful look and said, all in one breath, "Well, a thousand would be sweet, but I could get by with three or four hundred. I don't need it until next month. Say around the fifteenth? That'll give me enough time to finish the rest of my holiday shopping." She slightly turned her head and looked at me from the corner of her eye with a crooked smile on her face. What she said next made my chest tighten. "It's a shame you don't have a man to spend the holiday with, like other women your age." She paused and shook her head. "Boy, I wish you weren't going to Reno. Then the kids could spend Christmas Eve with you. We're coming home early on Christmas morning, so we'll be with them when they open all the nice gifts Santa is going to bring them."

I breathed a sigh of relief when Jim buzzed for me to come into his office before I could respond. "Uh-oh. I have to go. We'll have to finish this conversation later." I grabbed my steno pad and a pen and stood up.

There was a pout already on Debra's face. "Do you mind if I sit out here and wait for you to come back?"

I shook my head. "I'll probably be tied up for a long time. An hour or more," I predicted. She gave me a hug and rushed back to the elevator with the tails of her jacket flapping like bat wings.

Jim had buzzed me by mistake, so I was back at my desk within seconds.

When my parents returned from Carmel on Friday evening, I dropped by the home to hear about their latest jaunt. They raved about the restaurant where they'd eaten their meals and the celebrities they had seen. "One of our waiters showed us where Clint Eastwood sat the last time he came in. We snapped a bunch of pictures of that table," Daddy said, sounding as giddy as a young boy.

I could see that they were tired, so I didn't plan on staying long. But each time I attempted to leave, one or both thought of "one more thing" they needed to mention. "If you don't mind, I'd love a back rub before you go," Mama said. After that, I turned down their beds and trimmed Daddy's toenails.

"I'll be back in a day or so," I said on my way out,

rushing before they could think of something else for me to do.

When I got home, I watched a couple of movies before I finally went to bed around midnight. I didn't sleep long, though. I opened my eyes three hours later. I couldn't get back to sleep, so I got up and shuffled into my guest bedroom where I kept my computer. I had more than a dozen new e-mail messages. The only reason I decided to answer them later in the day was because I didn't want the recipients to wonder why I was up doing e-mail at such an ungodly hour.

Even though I was not sleepy, I returned to bed. I planned to stay as busy as possible to keep myself from dwelling on the fact that I would be spending Christmas alone this year—and not in Paris.

My life had become so humdrum, I was ready for something—anything—to happen that would shake things up for me. Little did I know, that was going to start in a few hours. . . .

CHAPTER 5

When I got up at eight a.m. Saturday morning, rain was thumping on the windows of my second-floor apartment like little rocks. That was one of the reasons I was still in my bathrobe and slippers two hours later when somebody knocked on my front door. I assumed it was one of my neighbors in the building because anybody else would have called before coming, and I would have had to buzz them in.

I looked through the peephole and saw a face I didn't recognize. One thing I never did was open my door to a stranger: male or female, day or night. I'd read about people who had done that and been pepper-sprayed, attacked, robbed, or all three. "Who is it?" I used the same curt tone I used when I had to deal with pesky telemarketers and overly aggressive salespeople. It never failed to discourage them.

"I'm looking for Vanessa Hayes," came the meek reply.

"What is this regarding?"

"I came to deliver a piece of her mail that the mailman accidentally left in my mailbox."

I slowly opened the door. Standing in front of me was a slim woman who appeared to be in her early forties. She had long, thick, black hair, and small brown eyes on a honey-colored face. Despite the weary look in her eyes and the dark circles underneath them, she was still pretty. "I'm Vanessa Hayes," I said in a much softer tone.

"I hope I'm not disturbing you," the woman said, looking me up and down. She wore an expensive-looking beige pants suit underneath a see-through raincoat, and she was holding a large umbrella.

"No, you didn't."

"I don't know when your mail was left in my mailbox. I had to go out of town for three weeks and just returned last night." She smiled and reached into her denim purse and pulled out a large white envelope and handed it to me. "I had put in a request at the post office for them to hold my mail, but they still sent something through that doesn't even belong to me."

I immediately noticed the official-looking return address. "This must be my passport! I applied for it weeks ago!" I exclaimed. I didn't know why I was standing in my doorway on a rainy Saturday morning telling a total stranger my business. Since she looked like she was interested, I kept talking. "I was going to reapply, but I was told that I probably wouldn't receive it in time for my vacation next month."

The woman sighed and shook her head. "Hopefully, you can still go now."

I shook my head. "I've already canceled my travel arrangements."

"I'm sorry to hear that. Anyway, I'll be on my way—"

I held up my hand. "Wait. Let me give you gas money for bringing this to me."

"No, that's not necessary," she said, shaking her head. "I have a few other errands to take care of today, so it was no problem." Then she gave me a puzzled look. "What I don't understand is how your mail ended up in my area. I have received other folks' mail before, but they all live on my street or close by. I was surprised to see something for someone who resides on Alice Street."

"Where do you live?"

"Webb Street."

"That's on the other side of town."

"I'm sorry I couldn't get it to you in time for your vacation." The woman gave me another smile and turned to leave.

"Um, what's your name? I really appreciate your thoughtfulness and would love to compensate you in some way."

"My name is Judith Ann Guthrie-Starks." She chuckled. "I know that's a mouthful, but I didn't want to give up my daddy's name just because I got married. He was from the UK and a lot of the women over there hyphenate their last names, married or not."

"That's interesting. Is that where you're from?"

"No, it's not. My father's family moved to London from Jamaica when he was a child. The company he worked for transferred him to California. My brother and I were born here. However, when we were children we spent every summer in London with my uncle and his family. It's a wonderful place and I have a lot of family and friends still there."

"My mother used to work for an airline, and she loved her stopovers in London." I was really enjoying this impromptu conversation, so I went on. "As much as she enjoyed her job, she retired five years ago so she could spend more time with my father. He'd already retired a couple of years before."

Judith tilted her head to the side and chuckled again. "What a coincidence. My mother was a flight attendant for fifteen years. When my father died two years ago, she moved back to London. She passed last year."

"I'm sorry for your loss. Would you like to come in for a cup of coffee?" I felt comfortable and wanted to chat some more. The rain had made me feel gloomy, so this was a welcome diversion. I opened the door wider and motioned for Judith to enter.

"No, thank you!" she exclaimed, shaking her head. "I have a busy day planned, so I really must be going. Good day."

Before I could say another word, Judith spun around and padded down the hall.

The second I closed the door, my landline rang. It was Madeline. "You ignored the message I left on your cell phone last night," she accused.

"Sorry. I went to visit my folks after I got off work. It was kind of late when I got home."

"I would give anything in the world to have my folks closer. It's hard to believe they moved to Florida three years ago," Madeline said with a heavy sigh. But her tone perked up so quickly, it startled me. "Kirk is taking the kids to Berkeley to spend some time with his folks, so I'm at loose ends. Let's go shopping. We can have lunch and get our nails done, too."

"I don't want to go out in this nasty weather. I just got over a cold," I said as I plopped down on the couch.

"Okay, but don't get mad when you hear about all the nice pieces I picked up today. That boutique on Willow Street is having a going-out-of-business sale and I want to get there before all the good stuff is gone."

"I don't need any new clothes. I have items in my closet with the tags still attached from the numerous going-out-of-business sales we've been to this year. If you find something I like, I can always borrow it from you, like I always do," I chuckled. I cleared my throat. "Listen, I just had an interesting encounter."

"Please tell me Barry hasn't had a change of heart and now wants—"

I cut Madeline off. "My passport ended up in another woman's mailbox and she just delivered it."

"So? What's so interesting about that? My neighbors' mail ends up in my box from time to time, and vice versa."

"The odd thing is, this woman lives across town on Webb Street. You've been supervising mail processing at the post office for five years. Do they make mistakes like this often?"

"Everybody makes mistakes. Even us postal workers," Madeline said, sounding slightly defensive. "But your mail being delivered so far away is odd. It's the first time I've ever heard of something like this happening. Well, at least you received your passport in time for your vacation."

"I didn't think I would, so I canceled it on Monday. I'll have to visit Paris some other time."

Madeline took her time responding. "V, what if that mail mix-up wasn't a mistake and your passport was supposed to end up with that woman?"

"That's ridiculous. Why would that be?"

"Well, they say everything happens for a reason."

"You sound like Mama. That's one of her favorite sayings."

"Maybe you *had* to cancel because something more important is going to happen in your life that you need to be here for."

"Well, whatever it is, I can't wait for it to happen."

CHAPTER 6

It had been an hour since the stranger dropped off my passport, and I was still thinking about her. My curiosity got the better of me and I wanted to know more about Judith Guthrie-Starks. Before I turned on my computer to Google her, I decided to check the telephone book first. She was listed. Without giving it much thought, I dialed her number. The telephone rang six times before she answered. "Hello. May I speak with Judith?" I began, using the gentlest tone I could manage. Especially because of the harsh way I'd first greeted her this morning.

"This is she. Who's calling?"

"This is Vanessa Hayes. I'm sorry to bother you at home, but I just wanted to thank you again for bringing my passport today."

"It was not a big deal. I was glad to do it," she replied. "At least now you won't have to wonder what happened to it."

"I really enjoyed talking to you. I would still like to treat you to a coffee break or buy you lunch."

"I could definitely use a break," Judith said. She sounded tired, so I didn't want to keep her on the phone too long. However, I was eager to get together with her in person.

"I'd like to hear more about London. It's one of the places I plan to visit someday."

"Despite the dreary weather, it's a lovely town. I'm sure you'll love it." She didn't sound so tired now. "I've got tons of stories to share about London. When would you like to meet up?"

"How about later today if you're not too busy? I could come now. I got your address out of the phone book. Even though it's kind of nasty outside, I'd love to get out of my apartment for a little while. I know all the nice cafés in town—some are in your neighborhood." I suddenly felt guilty about turning down Madeline's invitation to go shopping and almost changed my mind about visiting Judith. But I was so curious about her, I had to go through with it.

"If you don't mind, it would be better if you came to my place. I'll explain why when you arrive. I still have a couple of errands to run. Can you come in an hour or so? The security code you'll need to press to get into the building is zero-four-four. I'll see you then."

To kill time, I went to the car wash, got some gas, and did a little window shopping at the strip mall along the way. It was nice to see all the businesses gearing up for Thanksgiving, which was my second favorite holiday next to Christmas. The furniture outlet at the corner had placed a table outside in front of the entrance. There was a scarecrow sharing it with a huge turkey piñata. The liquor store next door to it had real bales of hay piled up near their front door.

Shortly after I left the mall, I parked in front of Judith's three-story limestone building. It was on a wide street with an island in the middle lined with palm trees and exotic plants I'd never seen before. South Bay City was a small town located about twenty-five miles from San Jose. Judith's residence was located in an upscale area with a lot of old Victorian houses and well-kept apartment buildings.

She was standing in her doorway when I got off the elevator and still had on the same outfit she'd worn to my apartment. "I made brownies, so I hope you're not dieting," she said with a grin.

"I am, but I cheat once in a while," I confessed.

I was impressed when I entered her spacious living room. My apartment seemed so basic and ordinary compared to hers. Even though I kept everything neat and clean, almost everything I owned had come from IKEA and other discount stores, including the blue velvet couch I'd picked up at Goodwill. I had a few fake plants, a slightly scarred coffee table with mismatched end tables, a medium-size TV, and a lopsided, four-shelf bookcase, with my books in no particular order. Judith's place looked like a display room in a trendy furniture store. A brown leather love seat with a matching couch sat next to a huge flat-screen TV on a bronze metal stand. African artwork dominated every wall, along with framed pictures, including one of her sharing a table with Mick Jagger, with his arm around her shoulder.

"That photo was taken in London twenty years ago. Michael—we call Mick by his real name—used to visit a pub near my uncle's place and he was always eager to connect with his fans in public." She took my jacket and umbrella, waved me to the couch, and then she plopped down on the love seat across from me. "I've changed a lot since then."

"So has Mick," I pointed out.

"Touché," Judith agreed.

I exhaled and looked around the room. "You have a nice place, Judith. You've decorated it beautifully."

She beamed as she told me her husband was the one who had decorated their apartment. I was intrigued when I heard that his parents were missionaries who traveled all over Africa and Asia. "They send relics and other knickknacks to us all the time." She beamed even more when she revealed that her husband was a career marine. "He's only home a few weeks at a time. Then he gets deployed for several more months. He just left last month, so I won't see him again until May. Our son Paul is studying at Howard. He was born on our first wedding anniversary. Are you married?"

I cleared my throat and answered in a low tone, "Not yet." With a heavy sigh and a chuckle, I added, "I haven't had much luck in the romance department."

"Well, despite what we hear and read, there are a lot of nice men out there."

She excused herself and left the room to go get the coffee and brownies. While she was gone, a young, light-skinned man wearing a blue bathrobe and slippers shuffled into the living room. He stopped in the middle of the floor and stared at me with his eyes squinted. He was of medium height and weight, and even with dark circles around his glassy eyes, chapped lips, and his thick black hair askew, I could see that he was quite handsome. "You must be Vanessa Hayes," he said in a raspy tone of voice.

I stood up and extended my hand to shake his. He had big, strong-looking hands, but it felt like I was shaking a wet noodle. "Yes. The mailman accidentally left my passport in Judith's mailbox. She was kind enough to deliver it to me this morning. I offered to take her to lunch, but she wanted me to come here instead."

"She told me," he said, breathing through his mouth. Each breath made a rattling sound.

Immediately after he started coughing, Judith returned with a tray and stopped in her tracks as soon as she saw him. "Ronald, what are you doing out of bed?" she gently asked. "Dr. Thomas said you should stay off your feet as much as possible."

"I just wanted to stretch my legs," he replied in a whiny tone.

"Vanessa, this is my brother, Ronald," Judith introduced. "He's been staying with me for a while. Let's get you back to bed." She set the tray on the oval-shaped, smoked-glass coffee table, grabbed her brother's hand, and led him back out of the room. I poured myself a cup of coffee and started munching on one of the brownies. Judith returned five minutes later and sat back down on the love seat. "I'm sorry, Vanessa. It's been a very trying time for me lately."

"I understand. Is your brother very sick?"

Instead of answering right away, she stood back up and started shaking her head and wringing her hands. Before I realized what was happening, she burst into tears and stumbled over to the couch. She muttered some gibberish, her legs buckled, and she fell sideways onto the couch. I was flabbergasted to say the least. When I helped her sit up, I put my arms around her and rubbed her back. "It's okay, Judith. Go ahead and let it out."

She abruptly stopped crying after about a minute and scooted a few inches away. In a hoarse whisper she told me, "I don't expect him to be around much longer. . . ."

CHAPTER 7

Judith's words slammed into my ears like fists. I'd only lost a few elderly relatives and church family members, so I had not experienced as much grief as some of the people I knew. I couldn't imagine losing my parents or one of my siblings. I knew that when and if they departed before I did, the pain would be unbearable. The only thing I could think of to say was, "I am so sorry."

She grabbed a napkin off the tray, wiped her eyes, and honked into it. "I am so sorry for falling apart like this and soiling your blouse." She sniffled and dabbed the tears she'd left on my sleeve. "I'll pay for the dry cleaning."

"Don't worry about it. It's not a big deal," I assured her. "And this old blouse is hand washable."

An awkward moment of silence passed before Judith's demeanor changed so abruptly it made my head spin. It was hard to believe that a woman who had looked so woeful a few moments ago was grinning like a Cheshire cat now. "I'm so glad you came." She shifted in her seat and seemed to be more relaxed. "Let's get better acquainted. What type of work do you do?"

I told her about my job and a few other things about myself. I was impressed to hear that she was a teacher. "What school?" I asked.

"I taught phys ed at a private school in San Jose up until I joined the staff at South Bay City High five years ago."

"What a coincidence! That's something else we have in common. I graduated from SBC High, class of 2000. My last boyfriend used to teach math at a middle school in San Jose."

"Oh really? Do you still communicate with him?"

I shook my head. "We had a lot of fun and I cared about him, but we had too many obstacles to overcome. Going our separate ways was the best thing for us to do. I don't mind being on my own, though. I have a lot of interests, so I lead a busy life."

"I have a lot of interests, too, but taking care of my brother is my primary concern at the moment. Ronald is receiving dialysis treatments, but he still needs a lot of additional care. The school's been great. I've been on leave for two months and they still pay me a portion of my salary, but that's eventually going to end, and I'll have to return to work. Thank God,

Ronald has amazing health care insurance. It covers the bulk of his expenses. And, my husband has been in the military so many years, they pay him quite well. So long as we manage our money properly, we won't have to worry about finances for a while."

"I'm glad to hear that. Um . . . you mentioned dialysis treatments. Isn't that for someone who has problems with their kidneys?" I hoped that I didn't sound dumb. But I'd only heard of such treatments being associated with kidneys.

Before answering, Judith poured herself a cup of coffee and took a long pull. And then she leaned back in her seat and gave me the most woeful look I'd ever seen. "Six months after Ronald turned thirty last year, he suddenly began to get confused at the drop of a hat. And then he would get so tired, he could barely stand. He retained fluids, so there was some swelling in his feet, legs, and face. That quickly tapered off, so he didn't get too concerned." She exhaled and shook her head. "He hates going to the doctor. But when he got so weak he couldn't even function properly, he finally made an appointment. The news was not good. His ureter had narrowed. It's a genetic defect and it causes urine to back up in the kidneys. To make a long, painful story short, that led to kidney damage."

It was obvious that Judith was under a lot of stress. I could tell that she wanted to keep talking about her brother, so I didn't attempt to change the subject. I was glad to hear that he had a good job and owned a nice house not far from her residence. Rather than let the house sit empty, he'd arranged for one of his friends to move in until he could return. The rent he collected covered the mortgage, so that was one less thing for them to worry about. "There are days when I am so overwhelmed, I don't get much sleep," she said with a yawn.

I said the most appropriate thing I could think of. "Well, I'll leave so you can get some rest." I set my cup on the coffee table and stood up.

Judith held up her hand. "No, don't go! I'm really enjoying your company. I don't get to go out much and I don't like to entertain too often. What we're going through makes a lot of folks uncomfortable. Besides, everybody I know works and they have their own lives to attend to."

I sat back down. It made me feel good to know that my presence made Judith feel better. "Well then, I'll stay a little while longer." What I had heard so far had made me feel somewhat gloomy, but I was able to hide it. "Is anybody helping you take care of your brother?"

"Yes. We have relatives and friends who relieve me when they can. And a nurse drops in two or three times a week. Jan, my brother's fiancée, comes over several times a week." I was surprised to hear that Ronald was engaged. "She helped pick out the house they plan to raise their children in."

"That's nice," I mumbled. "Why didn't he get her to stay there instead of his friend?"

"He tried, but she said it would be too depressing to be there without him. Jan helps me out a lot. But it's so hard on her to see him hooked up to that dialysis machine." Judith sighed and glanced at her watch. "As a matter of fact, she should be here any minute now. She usually spends part of her weekends here. She was supposed to go to Long Beach with us. That's where Ronald and I were the past three weeks when the mail mix-up occurred. We have relatives down there." Judith paused and wrung her hands some more. When she started breathing through her mouth, I thought she was about to break down again. I was glad she didn't, because the way I was feeling, if she had, I would have shed a few tears myself. "He wants to visit as many of them as possible while he can still travel without a lot of discomfort. And, in case he doesn't get a kidney. As soon as we got the news about his condition, I immediately made arrangements to be tested. I was not a compatible match. Nor were any of the relatives and friends who volunteered to be tested. Jan was too afraid to consider being a donor. Her refusal stunned a lot of folks, especially Ronald.

If a man can't count on his own fiancée in a life-threatening situation . . ." Judith didn't finish her sentence. There was a grim look on her face when she spoke again. "In spite of the way Jan feels, she's a wonderful and caring person, and I don't blame her for not wanting to do it. She's an only child. It's a risky surgery and the consequences could be severe. If something were to happen to her, her parents would be crushed. That would kill Ronald, and me, too. She's probably not a match anyway. He's on a waiting list now. One that's quite long, I'm sorry to say."

"That's sad. I hope they find a kidney for him soon." I was really beginning to feel downhearted, so I knew it was in my best interest to leave in a few minutes. "Thank you so much for the coffee and brownies. If you need someone to talk to, just give me a call. And you're welcome to come to my place." I stood up again and retrieved my jacket from the coatrack. "I'm sorry I can't stay longer. Let's talk again soon."

Judith looked so glum when I walked toward the door. I felt guilty about leaving. It was obvious she still wanted to talk. If I hadn't left when I did, there was no telling how much longer I would have sat there listening to her painful story.

On my way home, I stopped at Walmart to pick up a few items. McDonald's was in the same vicinity, so when I finished shopping, I grabbed a burger. The way I was feeling now, the last thing I wanted to do was cook dinner.

After I'd devoured my Big Mac, I called up Anna. She'd left a message to let me know that the Lifetime channel was going to rerun a movie later tonight I had missed a few nights ago. We chatted about a couple of things before I decided to tell her everything that had transpired since Judith dropped off my passport. I even told the part about her literally crying on my shoulder, and Ronald receiving dialysis treatments.

"My goodness! What a day you've had. Are you going to keep in touch with this woman?"

"Yes, I am. It may help her deal with her situation a lot easier."

After my conversation with Anna ended, I took a long bubble bath and answered a dozen e-mails. When I returned to my living room, I noticed the message light blinking on my landline on the end table at the end of the couch. The only people who called me on my landline were telemarketers, wrong numbers, spam callers, and the few people who didn't have my cell phone number. I was surprised to see Judith's name and number on the caller ID. She'd left a message an hour and a half ago to let me know I'd left my umbrella at her apartment. I dialed her number right away. Before I could ask if it was okay for me to retrieve it tonight, she said sharply, "Vanessa, I'm sorry. You can't come back tonight. I'm on my way out the door. I need to get Ronald to the hospital right away!"

"Oh no!" I wailed. "Call me back when you get home. No matter how late it is." I immediately got a headache and a sick feeling in the pit of my stomach. I stayed up until midnight, hoping Judith would call again before I turned in for the night. When another two more hours went by and she hadn't called, I finally went to bed.

When I got up before dawn Sunday morning, I did as much as I could to keep myself busy so I wouldn't think about the distress my new friend was experiencing. I didn't have much of an appetite, so I didn't bother to eat breakfast. I considered staying home from church. I dismissed that thought because I knew if I did, I'd pace around and stare at my telephone until I heard from Judith.

CHAPTER 8

Some people who lived in other states thought that California was sunny all year. That may have been the case in the southern part of the state, but up north it got pretty cold in November. When I got up to get ready for church Sunday morning, it was so chilly, I had to turn on my heat. After I'd drunk two cups of coffee, I put on one of my long-sleeved cotton dresses and one of the two wool jackets I owned.

During the drive to church, I couldn't stop thinking about how frantic Judith had sounded on the telephone last night. There was not much I could do until I heard from her again. The best thing I could do for the time being was pray for her and her brother.

I loved New Hope Baptist Church. I'd been a member all my life. But now that I was grown and had so many other things going on in my life, I didn't attend every Sunday. Some days I just didn't feel like going, but I was always there in spirit. It was a small church always in need of a few minor repairs, but that didn't bother the fairly large congregation. And it was in a location convenient for everybody. Folks who didn't drive could take a bus that would let them off at the corner. There was a strip mall two blocks away, so after services ended (and sometimes during), several members of the congregation would do some shopping. We had a great choir and every event was always well organized and on time. My church family meant almost as much to me as my real family.

I was surprised not to see Mama and Daddy in attendance today, dressed up in colorful outfits looking like piñatas. Especially since they lived so close to the church. My siblings were also members, but they only showed up once or twice every other month. Odette and Madeline were Methodists, so they belonged to a different church. I occasionally visited theirs and they visited mine.

I had so much on my mind today, it was hard to concentrate on Reverend Jackson's sermon. I couldn't wait for him to finish. When he did, I had to endure our long-winded choir. They never sang less than eight hymns in a row.

When Reverend Jackson finally excused the choir and began mingling among the congregation, I took him aside the first chance I got. "I know you always have a lot of prayer requests, but I have a special one myself today," I blurted out.

He reared back on his stubby legs and folded his arms. "Oh? And what might that be?" he asked with his thick gray eyebrows furrowed. Each time he blinked, they wiggled. He was close to eighty, but still one of the most robust and vigorous preachers I knew.

"I don't know all the details, but I have a new friend who is taking care of her baby brother, who is seriously ill. She had to rush him to the hospital last night. I haven't heard from her since, so I don't know the status of his condition at the moment. But could you get the congregation to say a special prayer for them?"

Reverend Jackson massaged my shoulder and gave me a warm smile. "I'd be glad to. In the future, let me know somebody needs assistance before I start my regular sermon so we can get the prayers going sooner. Do you know the nature of the young man's illness?"

"He needs a new kidney or he'll die," I said quickly.

Reverend Jackson's eyes got big. "Good gracious! That's a mighty big order, but nothing is too big for God. Don't you worry about a thing, Vanessa. We got this one, praise the Lord."

"His name is—"

He held up his hand. "You don't need to tell me anything else. God knows who he is."

After I left church, shortly before noon, I joined Odette and Madeline in a back booth at Minnie's Coffee Shop, a block from my apartment. This was a once or twice a month ritual we'd started several years ago. It was one of the few times during the week when all three of us had free time. Madeline's two preteens, a boy and a girl, were still in Berkeley with her husband and in-laws. Odette's two teenage daughters were attending a birthday party at Round Table Pizza for one of their friends.

Madeline and Odette had dressed warmly, too. Madeline had on a turtleneck sweater and a floor-length skirt. Odette wore a thick shawl over her long-sleeved denim dress.

"Vanessa, I'm sorry you had to cancel your vacation, but is there something else going on with you? I've never seen you looking so gloomy," Madeline commented, ten minutes after I'd told them I wouldn't be going to Paris for Christmas. Madeline was the most attractive woman I knew. Her honey-colored complexion was so flawless, the only makeup she ever wore on her heart-shaped face was a little mascara. But she didn't even need that to look glamorous. Madeline was one of the lucky petite women who didn't exercise much, could eat whatever she wanted, and still never gain an ounce. "What else is bothering you?" she asked.

Odette shifted in her seat and raked her fingers through her short, bleached blond hair. She didn't wear much makeup either, only a little foundation and lipstick. She and I had to work out regularly and watch what we ate to keep our weight under control. "Yeah. You can't be that depressed about not going to Paris." She added more cream to her coffee and took a long pull.

There were several donuts on the table, but Madeline was the only one who was eating. I took a sip of my decaf before I answered. "I'm still a little bummed out about it and I'll start making plans to go next Christmas in a few weeks," I responded. "But I do have other things on my mind right now."

"Is it the promotion?" Madeline asked. "I sure hope Jim gives it to you. You'd make a great office manager. You might lose a few friends at work, though. It's hard to be chummy and firm at the same time. A good office manager has to really crack the whip to be effective. Especially with people like that Dennis. He's used to doing whatever he wants, whenever he wants. Maybe you should give it a lot of thought before you accept it."

I slumped down in my seat and blew out a loud breath. "One of the guys in the finance department got the promotion. Jim told me before I left work on Friday."

"Oh no, he didn't pass you over!" Madeline hollered.

"Humph! I guess Jim is not the best boss in the world like we all thought he was," Odette griped.

"I still think he is," I defended. "And for your information, he did offer me the job. I turned it down."

"You what?" Odette and Madeline yelled at the same time.

"I love being his executive assistant. I have a lot of flexibility and there is no pressure. Besides that, I already make almost as much as the office manager position," I explained.

"But you've been doing that job for so long. Don't you think it's time for a change?" Odette said in a loud tone.

I shook my head. "My daddy used to say, 'If something is on the right track, don't send it on a detour.'" I chuckled. "Besides, I'm not interested in supervising ten people, especially the ones who have been with the company a lot longer. It would be too stressful. The man who left the position started with a full head of jet-black hair five years ago. When he resigned last month, the few strands he had left were all snow white. Poor Grant. The week after we had his farewell party, he started seeing a psychiatrist. I don't want to end up like that."

"Tell me about it. I love being a nurse but there are

times when I wish I had chosen another profession,"
Odette admitted. "I lost two patients last night. One
died right after his sister brought him in."

My jaw dropped and my eyes got big. "Was it a
man named Ronald Guthrie?" I asked. "His sister
told me he wasn't doing well and that she had to take
him to the hospital last night."

"No, it wasn't him," Odette replied. "But he was
admitted again last night, too."

"Who is Ronald?" Madeline asked.

I shared the whole story about my encounter with
Judith and Ronald yesterday. By the time I finished,
Madeline and Odette were staring at me with puzzled
looks on their faces. And then Madeline asked with a
grimace, "And you're already friends with these
strangers?"

"They're not really strangers anymore," I protested.

"Ronald and his sister are not strangers to me,"
Odette stated. "He's been one of my patients for several months now and I know him and Judith quite
well. They are very nice people. And he's so handsome. . . ."

Madeline suddenly got even more interested. She
leaned across the table and whispered, "V, if his
health improves, it might be worth your while to get
to know him better." With a sheepish grin, she added,
"Every woman needs a man."

I shook my head. "Not this one. He's probably not my type and he's a couple of years younger than me. I've never been involved with a younger man. Besides, I can be happy for the rest of my life without a man." I hated when other women made that statement. I immediately wished I could take it back. One reason was because I wasn't so sure it was true. . . .

CHAPTER 9

"*Two* years? Girl, please! You're not an old hag yet!" Madeline hollered. She lowered her tone when she saw people at the table next to us staring at her with amused looks on their faces. "Your own brother is seriously involved with a woman five years older than him!"

"Gary is very mature for a man his age," I shot back.

"How do you know that Ronald is not very mature for his age?"

"I don't know if he is or not. But his age is not the only issue. He's also engaged," I said.

"He's got his work cut out for him because she's very high maintenance. She's not even thirty and already owns a couple of successful beauty supply stores. And has even won a couple of beauty pageants," Odette said with a wistful look on her face. "Ronald is crazy about her."

"Really, Odette? How do you know so much about Ronald's fiancée? Do you know her?" I asked.

I couldn't believe we were discussing people I'd just met yesterday. But the subject was so intriguing to me, I wanted to discuss it some more. Judith had told me enough to gain my sympathy. But I wondered what she hadn't told me. Ronald was engaged to a beautiful and successful woman and that was a good thing for him. But there was no telling what she was really like. And, despite his medical condition, he could have been the boyfriend from hell for all I knew. And maybe his fiancée was staying with him out of pity or fear. However, something told me that wasn't the case.

I scolded myself for letting my thoughts run in such a negative direction. I had always given people the benefit of the doubt until they gave me a reason not to.

Odette rolled her eyes and gave me an amused look. "Yes, I've met Ronald's fiancée. When he nods off during one of her visits, she hangs around a few minutes longer and chats with me. Nurses are the new bartenders and hairdressers. People like to share their business with us."

"Amen," Madeline agreed. "I have an aunt who stopped going to her therapist when the advice she got from the lady who does her hair helped her work through her problems quicker and for a lot less money." She narrowed her eyes and whispered, "I thought you medical people weren't allowed to reveal your patients' personal information. Isn't there some kind of rule in place like there is with priests and lawyers?"

Odette snickered. "Pffftt! I haven't disclosed anything about Ronald, or any of my patients, that's not already public knowledge. His fiancée is at the hospital even more than his sister. He talks about her all the time. Every time she visits or calls, it lifts his spirits. But it's not doing much to help his overall health. He's a very sick man."

Although I had only been in Ronald's presence for a few moments, I cared about his well-being. Especially when I recalled how Judith had gone to pieces in front of me yesterday. "Judith thinks his situation is bleak. What do you think?" I asked Odette.

She looked keenly at me and inhaled with her mouth open. "When somebody needs a new kidney, that's as bleak as it gets. Otherwise, he will die," she said flatly.

Hearing that prognosis coming from Judith was one thing. Having it confirmed by someone with a medical background was even more disheartening. I should have steered the conversation in a more pleasant direction. But I was too curious to stop now. Besides, Odette didn't seem to mind answering my questions. "From a professional standpoint, if you don't mind sharing, what kind of timeline are we talking about—a few months, a year?"

Her eyelids fluttered and she gave me a woeful look. "I hate to say this, but if he doesn't get a new kidney in the next six months, he's probably not going to live to see next Christmas," she grimly predicted. "One day when his sister came to visit I overheard him telling her he wanted to update his will and pay off all of his bills ASAP." Odette let out a mournful sigh and shook her head. "I feel so sorry for that poor woman. He's her only sibling. You and she really hit it off, right?"

"Yes, we did. I really like her and wouldn't mind getting to know her better. It was so thoughtful of her to bring my passport to me. We had a really nice long chat at her apartment yesterday afternoon." I shared some of the interesting things Judith had told me. "It seemed like my visit did her a lot of good." I didn't want to tell them about her tearful breakdown. If I thought it was an odd way for a woman to behave with a virtual stranger, I knew they would, too. The last thing I wanted was for them to try and discourage me from getting too close too soon. "Maybe I can help keep her brother's spirits up. I hope he's well enough to come home soon. I'd really like to know him better."

"Do you think it's a good idea to get close to some-body who might not be around much longer?" Madeline asked.

Odette's jaw dropped. "What's the matter with you, Madeline? That's such an insensitive thing for you to say," she scolded. "Each day is important, no matter how many more we have left."

Madeline gave me an apologetic look. "I know, and I'm sorry for asking such a thoughtless question. V, do you want me to go with you the next time you visit Judith? I would like to meet her and Ronald my-self."

"Maybe after I get to know them better. Judith told me she didn't like having company too often, so bringing someone with me too soon is probably not a good idea," I replied.

"True. But if I had their problems, I'd want as much support as possible," Odette said.

"I would too," I admitted.

We finished our coffee and discussed work and a few other subjects before we left. When I got back to my apartment, I returned a few phone calls and checked my messages before I shoved a frozen TV dinner into the oven.

Judith called me up four hours later. I was glad to hear that Ronald was no worse, and that she was in a much better mood. It was a brief conversation and I didn't think to ask when I could retrieve my umbrella until we had ended the conversation. I didn't want to wait too late to call her back, so I called right away. Another woman answered in a gruff tone and it startled me. "Y-yes, may I speak to Judith?" I stammered.

"She's not available at the moment," the woman said curtly. "Who's calling?"

"I'm Vanessa, Judith's friend." As an afterthought, I added, "And Ronald's."

"Oh? I'm Jan, his *fiancée*." I couldn't understand why she thought it was necessary to put so much emphasis on who she was to Ronald. "Have I met you before?"

"No, I just met Judith and Ronald yesterday. I don't know if they've mentioned me, but my name is Vanessa Hayes."

"They haven't," she said sharply. "Look, this is not a good time. Can you call back some other time?"

"Of course." I hung up immediately and called Odette. She didn't answer, so I tried Madeline's number. She answered right away. I said, "I just had an odd conversation."

"Oh? Does it have anything to do with your passport and that woman and her sick brother?"

"Well, yes. I talked to Judith a little while ago and I was pleased to hear that her brother is doing okay for now. Anyway, I left my umbrella at her place yesterday and I wanted to find out when I could go pick it up. Ronald's fiancée answered."

"So? What's so odd about that?"

"She was cold the minute she answered the phone, but she sounded downright irritated when I told her I was Ronald's friend."

"In the first place, you saw Ronald for a split second, only one time. Maybe you can call Judith a friend, but to say that he's your friend—to his fiancée at that—sounds a little too bold."

"Do you really think so?"

"Maybe that's not the right word. But put yourself in that woman's place. She's probably as stressed out as Judith is because of what's going on with Ronald. The last thing she needs to worry about is a woman she's never met referring to herself as her fiancé's 'friend.'"

"I see what you mean. It's no big deal, so I am not going to worry about it. I'll talk to you tomorrow." I hung up and started cooking the spaghetti I planned to have for dinner. After I'd eaten I washed my hair and checked to see what was on TV. Ten minutes into a rerun of *Dr. Phil*, my cell phone rang. It was Judith. I was glad I hadn't turned it off and that it was within reach, so I didn't have to get up.

"Vanessa, I apologize for calling so late. But I wanted to remind you about your umbrella. I didn't think about it until a few minutes ago."

"I realized that right after we hung up, so I called right back. Did Jan tell you I called?"

"She didn't mention it."

"Okay. I have more than one umbrella, so there is no rush for me to come get it."

"That's fine. I hope we can get together again soon. I don't want to spend all of my free time at the hospital or moping around the house. Maybe we can have dinner or check out a movie one day next week."

"I'd like that. I'm cooking a huge meal for Thanksgiving. My parents and one of my coworkers and her husband will be joining me. I'm sure they'd all love to meet you."

"Thank you so much, but I'll be eating dinner with Jan and some of her relatives. I'm hoping that they will release Ronald in time so he can be there, too. Before all this started, the two of them were inseparable. He's had a couple of other serious relationships, but they were not nearly as important as this one. Jan is his world."

"I'm glad to hear that," I mumbled. "Let's talk again in a couple of days. We can decide then about dinner and a movie."

I scolded myself for saying what I'd said about Jan to Madeline. If somebody as sweet and likable as Judith thought so much of her, and if she was Ronald's world, she had to be something special.

If Judith and I were going to become close friends, I hoped that Jan and I could become friends, too. I read somewhere that the Duchess of Windsor once said, "A woman can never be too rich or too thin." I think she should have also said, "And a woman can never have too many friends."

Anna Wong was one of my best friends and her opinions were important to me. That was why I called her after my conversation with Judith and told her everything that had transpired since yesterday. "I'm glad you were able to comfort Judith. But be careful. . . ."

"What's there to be careful about?"

"V, all I'm saying is don't get too emotionally involved too soon. You don't want Judith to become too dependent on you. It could cause all kinds of problems," Anna warned. "Remember that temp who got so attached to you last year because you consoled her when her husband ran off with another woman?"

"I'll never forget her," I replied with a groan. "I still shudder when I think about how even after her assignment ended, she'd still call me every hour on the hour every day and show up unannounced."

"If her husband hadn't taken her back when he did, you could have had a stalker situation on your hands."

"Pffftt. You are going way overboard. That was a totally different situation. All I'm doing is letting Judith cry on my shoulder. I don't see how that can lead to any problems."

"All you did for that temp was let her cry on your shoulder, too. The next thing I knew, she was carrying on as if you were her own personal therapist." I leaned back in my seat and listened as Anna rambled on with warnings and advice for five minutes. Even though her voice was thick with exhaustion, she paused for a few seconds and started up again. She finally concluded with, "Promise me you'll be careful, V."

"I promise."

CHAPTER 10

Each year, our office closed at noon the day before Thanksgiving and Jim gave us the Friday after off as well, with pay. Mama had cooked a huge feast last year and invited our family and people from church. She had also invited Barry, but he had to cancel and fly to LA to attend his grandfather's funeral, so I had gone to dinner by myself. This year was going to be very different. My sister and her family were going to spend the holiday with her in-laws, and my brother and his girlfriend were going to celebrate in Tahoe. So, it would just be myself, my parents, and Anna and her husband.

I had already purchased a medium-size turkey and a small ham, along with all the fixings. When I got off work on Wednesday, I stopped at the supermarket to pick up a couple of items I had overlooked. Mama made a fuss when I didn't have cranberry sauce, and

Daddy sulked if I didn't have apple cider, and it had to be organic.

I got up Thursday morning and started preparing the feast I'd been looking forward to for weeks. I had everything ready by noon, but I had told everybody we wouldn't eat until two p.m. When my phone rang a few minutes before that time, I assumed it was my parents calling to let me know they were on the way or running late. It was Judith.

"Vanessa, I'm sorry to be bothering you, but I couldn't reach anybody else," she said with her voice cracking. One thing was for sure, Judith was fragile. I couldn't imagine how she would be when—and if—her brother didn't make it.

"What's the matter?"

"It's my brother again."

"He didn't . . ." I couldn't even finish my sentence. My heart was beating so hard I had to rub my chest.

"He didn't die. But he really needs some emotional support right now and I am just about worn down to a frazzle."

"What happened?"

"Jan called off the wedding last night. She did it in an e-mail message to his cell phone! I can't believe somebody could do something that callous."

I couldn't believe my ears. Especially after Judith had made Jan sound so devoted. "Nothing surprises me these days," I admitted. "I hope he didn't take it too hard."

"He claims he's okay, but I know better."

"What was her reason? Is she no longer in love with him? Or is there someone else?"

"She still loves him. There is no doubt in my mind about that. I don't know if she's interested in someone else. She's never given me a reason to think that. After my last conversation with you, Ronald took a turn for the worse. He's doing better now. Things are still so grim his chances of living are even slimmer. I can understand how Jan's feeling. They were planning to get married on the beach in Jamaica next summer, start their family right away, and do everything else married couples do. I wasn't too hopeful about that anymore, but I believe Ronald and Jan thought there was a chance he'd make it. They were not being realistic, though. Ronald was doing better for a brief period of time, but his latest relapse was more than she could stand, I guess. She became so overwhelmed at the hospital the other day, she had to be tranquilized."

"I am so sorry. Are you still planning to eat dinner at her place today?"

"She and I didn't discuss it, but I'm not going. I don't think I can be around her for a while without breaking down myself. I . . . I can't understand why she couldn't tell Ronald to his face! Can you imagine someone ending a relationship in an e-mail, or any other way other than in person?"

"Um . . . that is pretty bad. I know how Ronald feels." I was glad Judith didn't ask me to elaborate. Just thinking about the break-up e-mail I had received from Barry sent a sharp pain through my chest. This was her pity party, so I didn't want to discuss it with her and divert the attention away from Ronald. "Would you like to come to my place for dinner today? We're planning to eat around two p.m., but if you can't make it by then, you can come when it's more convenient."

"Thank you, but I think I should spend time with my brother today. I'm going to leave for the hospital in a little while."

"If you change your mind, just give me a call. Listen, I'm not doing anything tomorrow, so we could get together then if you'd like. There will be plenty of food left over today, so I can fix you a plate."

"I'll call you later today and let you know. Thanks for listening again." Judith let out a long, loud breath. "Vanessa, I'm scared. And I don't care what my brother says, I know he's scared, too. One of our uncles came up from Jamaica recently to be tested to see if he's a compatible donor."

"That's wonderful! Do you think he could be?"

"I thought all the folks who got tested could be and they were not. We've been disappointed so many times, I don't know what to think anymore."

"When will you know if your uncle is a match?"

"Any day now. I'm so anxious to find out; I can barely stand it."

"Please keep me posted." I was about to end the call when I thought of something else I could do to make Judith and Ronald feel better. "Do you think he would mind if I came with you to visit him at the hospital?" I would never have suggested such a thing if Jan hadn't removed herself from the picture.

"Vanessa, I'd really like that. I'm sure Ronald would, too. But let's wait until after my uncle's test results are ready. If he can't be a donor, Ronald will be disappointed again and I'll need as much emotional support as I can get to keep him from sinking into the doldrums. Have a happy Thanksgiving. I'll still try to give you a call later in the day."

Ten minutes after my conversation with Judith, Anna called. "V, I am so sorry to do this to you. But Gus and I won't be able to make it to dinner today. He woke up with one of his migraines this morning. We thought he'd be okay in a few hours, but he's not. He's even worse," she wailed.

"That's too bad. Tell Gus I hope he feels better soon."

"We were really looking forward to enjoying a nice

dinner. Now I'll have to throw something together," Anna whined.

I was slightly disappointed. I had cooked a pot of collard greens as one of the numerous side dishes. But since Gus preferred turnip greens, I'd cooked a separate pot just for him. "Look, I will have plenty of leftovers. I can bring you and Gus a plate later today, or tomorrow."

"That would be so nice of you. But I don't want to inconvenience you. I'll come over tomorrow to pick it up. Bye now."

When I opened the door for Mama and Daddy five minutes after I got off the phone with Anna, the first thing he asked in a gruff tone was, "Why are you looking so gloomy today, sugar?"

"And on such a joyous day," Mama added. I was happy to see she didn't need her walker today.

"Anna had to cancel. Her husband is not feeling well," I explained. I hung up their coats and they plopped down on the couch.

"I hope it's nothing too serious," Mama said with a concerned look on her face. "This is the worst time of year for anybody to be sick."

"Another one of my friends has an even more serious situation to deal with. I was on the phone with her a few minutes ago and she was in a pretty sad state." I sat down in the wing chair facing the couch. "She felt better after I talked to her."

"Oh. Well, you young people are so resilient. I'm sure she'll bounce back soon. Which friend was it?" Mama said.

"Her name is Judith. My passport ended up in her mailbox by mistake and she brought it to me last Saturday morning. I visited her for a little while later that afternoon and we've talked on the phone a few times. We have so much in common, we've become friends already."

Daddy snorted and gave me a curious look. "What's the situation that's got this new friend of yours so down?" he asked.

I told them about Ronald and how taking care of him was taking such a toll on Judith. I even told them about Jan breaking up with him. When I finished speaking, my parents looked as bad as I felt. "That's a shame. With all the new technology and medicines they have today, you would think they'd have come up with another solution when somebody needed a new organ," Daddy commented. "And he's lucky that fiancée showed her true colors before he married her. Only a selfish, self-centered woman would turn her back on a man with all the misery he's got going on."

"That poor fellow. What a shame and a pity," Mama remarked. She stared at the floor for a few moments. When she looked up, she looked petrified.

That scared me. "Mama, what's wrong?" I asked with my heart racing. My mother was the kind of woman who only got distressed when something was extremely serious.

"It's nothing for you to worry about." She let out a weak chuckle and stood up. There was a tight smile on her face, but I knew her well enough to know that it was forced. "Enough talk." She looked toward the kitchen and sniffed. "Let's go eat!"

When we sat down at the table in my tiny dining area, I noticed that the same petrified look was back on Mama's face. Daddy was so busy carving the turkey he didn't notice it. Or maybe he'd seen it before but never mentioned it.

Mama occupied the seat across from me. When I attempted to touch her hand, she pulled it away. "Mama, did Dr. Cortez give you some bad news when you got your checkup on Tuesday?"

"Dr. Cortez thinks I'm in excellent shape for a woman my age. Now, stop asking me what's wrong," she said sternly. When she smiled this time, I knew it was for real. She scanned the food I had set on the table, smacked her lips, and looked at me in awe. "Baby, you really outdid yourself this time! I bet that turkey is so tender, I could eat it without my teeth."

"Mama, please don't remove your dentures like you did at last year's Fourth of July cookout," I pleaded with a shudder. We all laughed long and loud.

We didn't waste any more time talking before we piled food onto our plates. Other than a few compliments about my cooking, we ate in silence for the next ten minutes. After his third glass of cider, Daddy let out a mighty belch and excused himself to go take a bathroom break. "He always eats too fast when there is a lot of food in front of him. I hope I don't have to listen to him bellyache about a bellyache later today," Mama grumbled.

"Don't worry. I'll give him some Pepto Bismol in a little while." I had eaten too fast also, so I knew I'd be guzzling some antacid myself before the day was over.

After a long, loud sigh, Mama set her fork down and gave me a pensive look. "Sugar, are you still disappointed about not being able to go to Paris this Christmas?"

I shrugged. "I was for a little while. I'm fine now, though. I still don't understand how my passport accidentally ended up in the wrong mailbox."

"Maybe it wasn't an accident," Mama suggested.

I gave her an incredulous look. "Of course it was. Why would the post office send a piece of my mail to the wrong address on purpose? That makes no sense at all." I recalled how Madeline had made a similar remark. It didn't make any sense when she said it, and it wasn't making any sense coming from Mama.

"It's possible that the post office is not to blame. I've been telling you all your life that everything happens for a reason."

"I hope I find out that reason soon. One good thing that came out of it was that I met Judith and Ronald." I sighed. "I just wish it had been under better circumstances."

And then Mama said something with so much conviction, it threw me for a loop. "Your friend's brother is going to be just fine."

"You seem so sure."

"Don't look so skeptical. I am sure," was all she said. The next thing I knew, she went off on a verbal tangent about everything from the wonderful new inflammation gel she'd been using on her bad knee to praising Tyler Perry's last movie. I took this as a hint to stop talking about Ronald for now.

CHAPTER 11

After I had put away the leftovers and washed the dishes, I joined Mama and Daddy in the living room. We had coffee and watched a couple of Hallmark and Lifetime channel holiday movies I had previously recorded. I didn't notice any more disturbing looks on Mama's face. After the last movie ended, we called up a few out-of-town relatives and local friends to share our happiness about all the things we had to be thankful for this year. It turned out to be such a pleasant day, I didn't want it to end.

I tried to persuade my parents to spend the night with me, but they didn't waste any time letting me know that my bed was too lumpy for them and sleeping on a pallet on the floor was out of the question. They left a few minutes later.

I didn't hear from Judith that evening, so I called her Friday shortly before noon. My call went straight to voice mail.

I was tempted to call the hospital to see if she was with her brother, but I thought that would be a little too forward. I waited a couple of hours and called her number again and still got her voice mail. I decided to wait until I heard from her, but when she hadn't called me back by Sunday night, I made another attempt. I breathed a sigh of relief when she answered. "Judith, I just wanted to check in with you to see how Ronald is doing," I started.

"Pretty good under the circumstances. I apologize for not calling you back before now, but things have been pretty hectic since our last conversation. Our uncle's kidney is not a match!" she blurted out.

"Oh no."

"The doctor told us ten minutes after I got to the hospital on Thanksgiving Day. I would have called you before now, but I've been in a fog ever since. That bombshell, and the fact that Jan deserted him, would have destroyed any other person. But Ronald is taking these new developments in stride and is even more upbeat than usual."

"I'm glad to hear he's taking things so well. I doubt if he'd be able to do it without you," I said. "Do you want me to go with you when you visit him at the hospital the next time?"

"I'm bringing him home tomorrow. This seems like it's never going to end," Judith said with a sniffle. She sounded so defeated, I was beginning to worry about her health, mental and physical. If she gave up, where would that leave Ronald? I knew she was a strong woman, but how much more could she take before she went to pieces completely? I wondered.

"Then he must be doing better, right?"

"Just barely. His doctor has advised me to make him as comfortable as possible for as long as I can."

"It sounds like his doctor has given up hope," I said in a weary tone, with tears pooling in my eyes.

"Well, that's one way of looking at it. And I know Ronald has accepted his fate. But I'm having a hard time doing that myself. I...I...I'm going to lie down for a while. I haven't slept more than a couple of hours the past two days. I look forward to seeing you again. I promise I won't cry on your shoulder too much when I do."

"You can cry on my shoulder as often as you need to. I can come over tomorrow after I get off work. Call me when you get home from the hospital tomorrow. Is there anything you want me to bring? Groceries, or anything else?"

"No, I'm well stocked. But instead of coming tomorrow, wait a few more days. Some of Ronald's friends and coworkers are coming tomorrow and I don't think it'll be good for him to have too much company in the same day."

"Okay. Give me a call to let me know when to come."

I was glad Odette answered her phone when I called her right after I ended my conversation with Judith. Words started flying out of my mouth like torpedoes. I shared everything that Judith had told me. Odette couldn't get a word in until I had to pause to catch my breath.

"Oh my God, V. I didn't know about his fiancée ending their relationship or his uncle not being a compatible donor. I don't know how much more that poor man can endure before he truly gives up."

"I'm beginning to think he already has," I mumbled.

"I hope that's not true. I care about all of my patients, even though there are a few who really give me a run for my money. I get bedpans thrown at me, cussed out, and the other day one attempted to bite me when I gave him a shot. Ronald is the only one who never complains or gives any of the staff members a hard time. I wish I could do more to help him get through this nightmare."

"I think you're doing enough."

"I'd do even more if I knew what."

"Well, I'm sure that getting a new kidney is at the top of his bucket list. Would you be willing to give him one of yours?"

Odette gasped. "My God! I don't know about that."

"I feel the same way. I don't know if I could ever do something that serious for anybody," I admitted.

"I wouldn't hesitate to do it for one of my family members, especially my husband and my children. I adore Ronald, but he's not the only seriously ill patient I have that I feel close to. Two years ago, I had a twelve-year-old girl in need of a kidney. She reminded me so much of my daughters. I've had several others over the years; each case was equally serious. I've only got two kidneys, and even if I could choose one patient over another, which one would I choose? The little girl or the young father of six who was in my care at the same time? Fortunately for the father, a distant relative came through for him. He's been doing fine ever since."

"Did the little girl make it?"

"Yes, and in the nick of time. Everybody had been praying for a miracle and we received one. A young nun died in an automobile accident. The little girl got one of her kidneys and her other organs saved two other lives."

Odette had to cut the call short to go break up a dispute between her kids, but I still wanted to talk to somebody. Mama and Daddy didn't answer their phone and neither did Debra. Madeline did, but she was too busy to chat. The only person I was able to reach who had time to talk was my brother.

"Hey, sis. I was just thinking about you. I was going to give you a call," Gary claimed.

"I'll bet. How much do you need this time?"

"I don't need another loan. I just got a big raise. Now I can really start planning my future. Anyway, I was going to give you a call to see if you wanted to join Marlene and me for Christmas at her place. Debra told me yesterday that you had to cancel your trip to Paris and plan to drive up to Reno for the holiday. When I told Marlene, she screamed and told me to call you ASAP and invite you to join us." Gary and his girlfriend loved to entertain, and I'd enjoyed quite a few of their gatherings. But with all that was going on in my life, I didn't want to spend the holiday with a huge, boisterous crowd this year.

"Tell Marlene I said thanks, but I'd rather go to Reno."

After I ended my conversation with Gary, I got so antsy, I couldn't sit still. I didn't want to watch TV or call up anybody else, so I took a chance and decided to go visit my parents without calling first to make sure they were still up. It was only eight p.m., so I figured they would be. Daddy was in the recreation room playing cards with some of the other residents. Mama was watching TV. I dropped my jacket and purse onto the wing chair facing the couch where Mama was sitting. I eased down on the other end.

She had already put on her nightgown and turned down her bed. "I'm glad you came over, sugar. Alex usually plays cards for two or three hours and I get real lonesome."

"Mama, what's the matter? You have the same look on your face that you had when we had Thanksgiving dinner. And don't keep telling me nothing is wrong, because I know better." I was more determined than ever to find out what was bothering my mother.

Before I could get her to tell me, she gave me a sorrowful look and started talking with her lips barely moving. "Nothing is the matter with me." She stopped talking long enough to blow out a loud breath. "I can't stop thinking about that poor young man you told us about. Even though I don't know him, I feel so sorry for him."

I sighed and hunched my shoulders. "I barely know him myself, but I feel sorry for him, too."

"How is he doing now?" When I told Mama everything Judith had told me, she gasped and shook her head. "It's too bad his uncle's kidney didn't pass the tests. But there is still a chance that somebody else's will. God will make sure of that."

"I sure hope so, Mama."

"And I'm sure Ronald will get over that woman leaving him at such a critical time. Believe you me, he'll be much better off without her," she predicted.

"You're probably right. But we have to look at things from her perspective. I'm not sure I'd want to marry a man who might not be around long enough for us to have a family."

"Honey, I couldn't agree with you more. I . . . I . . . the only thing I think a person should take with them to the grave is their body."

Mama's last comment was so out of left field, it made my head spin. There was no way I was going to let her get away with not telling me what she meant.

CHAPTER 12

I cleared my throat and stared at Mama with my eyes narrowed. "What's that supposed to mean? And don't you dare tell me it means nothing! You're in good health, you have everything you've ever wanted, and you and Daddy will be around for a lot of years to come. What else could a person take to his or her grave other than their body, other than a deep dark secret?"

"I won't be taking any secrets with me."

"I didn't know you had any," I said meekly. The next thing I knew all kinds of thoughts formed in my head. What was my mother trying to tell me? My mind ran the gamut. Had I been adopted? Had she or Daddy been to prison? Did I have siblings I didn't know about? I was glad when Mama started talking again, because my head was about to split open from all the thoughts piling up in it.

"Well, it's not a secret, but it's something I've been reluctant to talk about." Mama cleared her throat and went on. "When you told me about your friend's brother, it brought back some painful memories. It's something that happened a long time ago. It's difficult to even think about, let alone talk about. I never saw any reason to bring it up. Until now." Mama shifted her position on the couch. She rubbed her bad knee and crossed her legs.

I was on the edge of my seat in a fever of anticipation. I was about to prod her along until she suddenly started talking in a low, controlled tone of voice.

"Several years before you were born, I was at death's door and was told that if I didn't get a new liver, I wouldn't live too much longer."

If I had been struck by a bolt of lightning, I couldn't have been more astonished. I scooted even closer to the edge of my seat. "What? Did you—what happened?"

"I'm still here, so obviously things worked out for me."

"How come you never told me? Have you shared this with Gary and Debra?"

"No, I haven't. I never wanted to talk about it with them either. My parents and a few other relatives and some of my church family were the only ones who knew. Oh, it was such a stressful time. A month after Alex came home from Vietnam, we got married. The following month I got so sick to my stomach, he had to rush me to the hospital. All three of my sisters had had similar symptoms with their first pregnancies. We believed that's all it was. But mine were more severe. We were all shocked and disappointed when the doctor told us I wasn't pregnant. They ran some tests and I can't tell you how distressed I was when they told me that there was a problem with my liver. I was told that if I didn't get a new one, I wasn't going to be around too much longer."

"My God. Who was your donor?"

"A young man who had died in a motorcycle accident. That's all I know about him, bless his soul. Even though I was happy, it saddened me to know that somebody else had to die for me to live. If I'd had a living donor, I wouldn't have felt so bad. If it had been the other way around, I would have donated one of my organs in a heartbeat. Giving somebody else the gift of life is a once-in-a-lifetime gift itself to everybody involved."

"So, basically, if you hadn't had the transplant, I wouldn't be here today?" My words sounded hollow and left a foul taste in my mouth.

"That's right. Even though my doctor told me I

could still have children, I was skeptical after so many years went by and I hadn't become pregnant. But I had so many other things to be thankful for. I loved being married to Alex and being a flight attendant. That's the only way we got to see so many different parts of the world. We kept ourselves as busy as we could because we never thought we'd have children. I can't tell you how happy I was when I found out I was pregnant with you. I was in my late thirties by then. We thought you'd be the only child we'd ever have, so I was totally stunned when Gary and Debra came along when I was in my forties. By then, all of my sisters and most of our friends had already become grandmothers."

I decided to say something to lighten the mood. "At the rate I'm going, I'll be old enough to be a grandmother by the time I have my first child, too." We chuckled.

Mama got serious again. "Don't even think like that. You're a nice-looking, smart woman, with a lot to offer. If you were a man, wouldn't you love to have a woman like you?"

"Well, yeah. I'm a pretty good catch, I guess," I agreed with a sheepish grin. Then I got serious again, too. "Are you ever going to tell Debra and Gary about your transplant? I think they have a right to know."

"Now that I've told you, I will definitely tell them. The only reason I brought this up was because of what you shared with us about your new friend and her brother."

"I'm glad you told me, Mama." Then, without hesitation, I said, "I'm going to get tested to see if I'm a suitable donor for Ronald."

Mama couldn't have looked more stunned if I had leaped off the couch and stood on top of my head. She gulped and stared at me with her mouth hanging open. "Did I hear you right? You want to donate one of your kidneys?"

"You heard me right," I said firmly.

She leaned toward me and squinted. "Vanessa, are you sure you really want to do something this serious?"

"Yes, I am. And didn't you just say that donating an organ so someone else can live is a once-in-a-lifetime gift?"

Mama coughed and rubbed her chest. "I did say that, and I meant it. But you're my baby girl! I don't want you to do something you might end up regretting," she said in a raspy tone.

"Why would I regret helping save somebody's life?"

"Honey, it's not that cut and dry. Nobody risked their life to save mine."

I folded my arms and crossed my legs. "Are you telling me you don't think I should do it?"

"No, I'm not. It's your decision. I am proud of the fact that you are willing to do something so noble. But I think you should give this a lot of thought before you commit yourself. Before you make your final decision, you need to discuss it with your daddy, and your brother and sister. And you might want to consider getting some input from Madeline, Odette, and Reverend Jackson."

"They'll probably try and talk me out of it. But I won't let them," I declared. "If I don't do it and Ronald dies, I'd spend the rest of my life wondering if I could have saved him."

Mama slid closer to me and covered my hand with both of hers. And then she started talking louder. "Vanessa, all I ask is that you give this a lot of serious consideration. Sleep on it for a while. At least a few weeks."

"Time is not on Ronald's side. I can't even begin to think about waiting 'a few weeks' to get this going. It'll take some time to get my test results back and that's even more time to consider."

Mama was squeezing my hand so hard it hurt, but I didn't mind. "Vanessa, you've been extremely generous to everybody all your life. Lending your car, or money and clothes to whoever asks, is one thing. You get those back. But once you give up your kidney, it'll be gone forever!" Mama stopped talking and gave me a pleading look. "This Judith woman must be desperate to ask you to do this. Just how well do you know her brother anyway?"

"She didn't ask me to do it. I've only spoken to her brother once. And it was just for a few moments."

Before I could continue, the front door eased open and Daddy strolled in, yawning and stretching his arms. Mama and I were still sitting on the couch. He sat down with a thud and a groan at the foot of his bed and kicked off his shoes. "It'll be a long time before I play gin rummy with that Barney Morris again. He skunked all the rest of us again. He got me for nine bucks! Humph, humph, humph. He's way too lucky," Daddy griped in the same breath. When he stopped talking, he looked from Mama to me with a curious expression on his face. "How come y'all sitting here acting like mutes? I could hear y'all yakking all the way outside. Who didn't ask you to do what, Vanessa? And who is Ronald?" he asked sharply. There was a worried look on his face by the time I'd told him everything I'd shared with Mama.

"I advised her to give this a lot of consideration," she said.

I held my breath. Daddy furrowed his brows and caressed his chin and said without hesitation, "Vanessa honey, if you think you can help this young man, do it. If it's meant to work out, it will."

"Thank you, Daddy." I breathed a sigh of relief. He still looked worried, but I was glad to see that Mama seemed more relaxed. "Maybe I shouldn't have said anything yet."

Mama gasped. "Why not?"

"For one thing, I may not even be a suitable donor and I would have upset everybody for nothing. Several people have been tested, including Ronald's sister and other blood relatives. The chances are even slimmer that I'll be a match."

"Who else have you told?" Daddy asked.

"Nobody. I just decided to do it a few minutes ago," I responded. "After Mama told me about her liver transplant."

Daddy shot Mama a hot look. "Ocie, you told me years ago that you never wanted to bring that up again!" he blasted.

"And I meant that. When Vanessa told me about her friend's brother, I felt it was time," she replied. "But now she's—" Mama stopped when I held up my hand.

"Let's end this conversation. I'm not going to mention this to anybody else until I get tested. I'll let Judith know, but I don't want Ronald to know because I don't want him to get his hopes up again."

"When do you plan to get tested?" Daddy gently asked.

I stood up and started easing toward the door. "As soon as possible. The sooner I get this over and done with, the better I'll feel." I paused long enough to put my jacket back on. "And, hopefully, so will Ronald."

CHAPTER 13

When I got home, I had messages from Odette and Madeline on my landline and cell phone, and a text from my sister. It was still fairly early, but I didn't want to call up anybody tonight. While I was fixing some tea, my phone rang. It was Madeline. "V, did you get my messages?"

"I just got home from visiting my parents a little while ago. I haven't listened to them yet."

"I called to confirm our plans for Tuesday night."

My memory was normally pretty good. But with so much on my plate lately, a few things had slipped my mind. "What plans?"

"You agreed to go to dinner with Kirk and me, and his brother, Homer. Don't tell me you forgot that already."

I had known Homer Lilly since he moved to the Bay Area from Bakersfield eight years ago. I'd always had a mild crush on him, but Madeline and Odette were the only ones I'd told. However, Homer had never attempted to have a relationship with me. One reason was because we'd never been available at the same time. Until now. But the timing couldn't have been worse. With the donor issue hanging over my head, romance was the last thing on my mind. "I thought we were going out next Tuesday?"

"When I asked you last week, this Tuesday was 'next Tuesday' and you said you'd love to go. You're the one who suggested that cute Italian restaurant on Barberton Street. This'll be the first time Homer did some socializing since his hip replacement surgery last month. He's really looking forward to it. And he loves Italian food, so I'm glad you picked Dino's."

I was hesitant, but I didn't want to disappoint Madeline or Homer. "Okay. What time?"

"Our reservation is for seven. Homer is riding with us, so do you want us to pick you up, too?"

"If you don't mind, I'd rather drive my own car and meet you guys there. That way, if things don't go well, I can leave when I want."

"Come on now. Don't be so negative. That's not like you at all. I thought you liked Homer."

"I'm just teasing. I do like Homer. I'll stay for the whole time. But I still want to drive my car."

"That's fine with me," Madeline said with a sigh of relief. "This will be fun for all of us. Kirk and I haven't been out in a while. Besides, Homer's been badgering us since Barry took off to arrange a blind date for him with you."

"I wouldn't call this a 'blind date,' because I've known the man for years. And to be honest with you, the crush I had on him for so long is not as strong as it used to be. Besides, I'm leery about a man who couldn't pick up the phone and call me himself and ask me out," I chuckled.

"Maybe he was too shy," Madeline suggested.

I heaved out an exasperated sigh. I refused to believe that a thirty-five-year-old man who'd already been married three times could be even mildly shy. "Yeah, right. I'm sure you and I will talk before Tuesday, but if something comes up and I have to cancel or postpone, I'll let you know as soon as possible."

"What could come up?"

"Well, I could get sick, or something else could come up." I couldn't tell Madeline what I was planning to do before I told Judith. If the hospital could set me up to be tested on Monday or Tuesday, there was no telling how long it would take and how I'd feel afterward.

"Yes, you could get sick, but what is this 'something else' you're hinting at? Please tell me that if someone you like better asks you to go out on Tuesday, you won't dump Homer to go with him."

"Come on! You of all people know me better than that. That's something I would never do."

"Okay then. Let's not worry about something else coming up. But, if you do have an emergency that you really need to take care of, I'll understand. I'm sure Homer will, too. He's a sweet guy and you'd be good for him. And, for all we know, he could be the one you've been waiting for."

I went to bed right after my conversation with Madeline, but I couldn't get to sleep. When I checked the clock and saw that it was only a few minutes after ten, I decided to give Judith a call. I needed to get the ball rolling before I thought about it too much and changed my mind. Or let somebody talk me into changing my mind.

Judith answered on the first ring. After a deep breath, the words flowed out of me like spring water. "I'm sorry to be calling at this hour, but I need to discuss something very important with you," I told her.

"I rarely go to bed before midnight anyway," she told me. "What do you need to discuss?"

"I want to get tested to see if I'm a suitable donor for your brother."

She took her time responding. "Vanessa, are you sure this is something you want to do?"

"I'm very sure."

"There are numerous tests involved. And it could

take a while before we know if you're compatible. And time is extremely critical now."

"That's why I decided to call you tonight. I want to get this started as soon as possible. Please get in touch with Ronald's doctor tomorrow if you can and let him know."

"I will," Judith mumbled in a weary tone. I was surprised she didn't sound more excited. "What does your family have to say about this?"

"I've only told my parents. They have a few concerns, but they're behind me all the way. I'm not going to tell anyone else until I know if I'm a match."

"Well, with all due respect, I think it's important for my brother to know right away. And I want you to tell him." I hadn't expected her to say that.

"But if I'm not a match, he'll be disappointed—"

Judith cut me off. "Vanessa, even if you're not a match, it would do a world of good for Ronald's morale now just to know you've made this decision."

She told me that in addition to meeting with Ronald's doctor for the preliminaries, I'd also have to meet with the entire transplant team so they could walk me through the process in more detail. "I have to let you know now that the compatibility testing procedure is very extensive and grueling," she added. I was surprised and disappointed that she didn't sound more enthusiastic.

"I don't care. I still want to go through with it."

"All right. I'll get in touch with Dr. Thomas first thing tomorrow morning." She sounded more enthusiastic now and that made me feel better.

I went to bed shortly after we ended our conversation. But I slept less than three hours that night.

CHAPTER 14

When I woke the next day, I regretted not telling Madeline last night what I was planning to do. I had no idea how she and Odette were going to react when I told them, but it didn't matter. I had already made up my mind. However, after I'd given my decision a little more thought, I wanted to know what other people close to me thought before I went through with it. So, right after our weekly Monday morning staff meeting, which included a ten-minute video of Jim roaming around one of our job sites in a hard hat and an orange vest, I asked Anna to accompany me to the ladies' room.

After she leaned down and checked the stalls to make sure we were alone, she folded her arms and looked me straight in the eyes. "Okay, why were you so quiet in the meeting? You didn't even laugh at the silly video of Jim. What's going on?"

"Everything is fine," I replied. And then I added with my voice shaking, "I guess."

Anna gasped. "What's going on with you? And why are you sounding so weird? Does this have anything to do with Barry? Is he back in the picture and still trying to get you to move to Maine? Did he—"

I held up my hand to interrupt her. "I haven't heard from him since the day he dumped me."

"Okay. If this is not about Barry, who is it about?"

"That's what I'd like to tell you, but not here." I glanced toward the door. "Do you have any plans for lunch today?"

Anna gave me a puzzled look. "Hello? I have the same plans I usually have on Monday. Half-price burritos at Juanita's. That's how you and I usually start off our week, remember?"

"Oh yeah." I paused and checked my watch. "We'd better leave now, or we won't find a seat."

We arrived at Juanita's ten minutes later. There was a larger than usual crowd, so there were no seats available, so we got our orders to go. When we got back to the office, we headed for our break room. I was glad it was empty. As soon as we sat down and started gnawing on our burritos, I slid my chair closer to Anna and said in a low tone, "Remember that man I told you about who needs a new kidney? His sister and I have become quite close."

Anna stopped chewing and gave me a bewildered look. "I figured you would get close to that woman."

I gave her a dismissive wave. "She's got a lot of other friends and family, so I'm not the only one trying to keep her spirits up. You can forget about her becoming too attached to me."

"What about her brother? Did they find a donor yet?"

"That's what I hope to find out real soon."

Anna suddenly looked as concerned as I was. "Really? You told me he was on dialysis. I thought that was supposed to keep a person functioning indefinitely."

"Well, 'indefinitely' could mean a few days, weeks, or months. If Ronald loses his will to live, that could probably make his situation even more critical."

"Well, there's only so much that can be done."

I took a very loud and deep breath before I continued. "I'm going to get tested."

Anna's eyes got wide and her mouth dropped open. There was a wad of burrito still in her cheek. She chewed and swallowed it with such a huge gulp, her eyes crossed. "Tested for what? Are you telling me you're going to donate one of your kidneys?"

I nodded so vigorously my neck ached. "And don't you dare try to talk me out of it," I advised.

"Talk you out of trying to help save a man's life?

Pffftt!" Anna waved her hand and gave me an incredulous look. "Honey, that's the last thing I'd ever do. I think what you're going to do is so awesome! There should be more people in the world like you."

I was taken aback by her reaction. A huge smile formed on my face. "I . . . I am so happy to hear you say that!" I squealed.

"I don't know much about things like this, but I do know there are some risks. Remember my cousin Lillian who lives in Baltimore? You met her and her husband Alan at my Christmas Eve party last year."

"I remember her."

"Three years ago, Alan needed a new kidney and she gave him one of hers. They had tested a bunch of folks and she was the only one suitable."

"How is he doing now?"

"He is healthier than ever. Thank God." Anna choked on a sob and grabbed a napkin. "I'm sorry. I get emotional every time I think about Alan." She dabbed a tear from the corner of her eye. After she honked into the napkin and wiped her nose, she gave me a pensive look. "If you can help that poor man live a fairly normal life, even if it's for only a few more years, I say go for it. When are you going to get tested?"

"I'm going to the hospital with Judith this evening. I'll know more after I meet with the doctor."

"How does Ronald feel about all this?"

"Other than you and my parents and Judith, I haven't mentioned it to anyone else. I'll let him know this evening."

"What? You haven't even told Madeline or Odette?"

"I don't want to tell them until after my test results come back. And only if I'm a match."

"Why? Do you think they'll talk you out of going through with it?"

I shook my head. "Nobody is going to make me change my mind." I heard a cough. Anna and I turned around at the same time. Dennis was standing in the doorway with a can of Coke in his hand. "How long have you been standing there?" I asked.

"Long enough," he replied. He strode over to the table with a blank look on his face. "I heard everything, and I commend you."

"Dennis," I began, "I know you like to keep our coworkers informed about what's going on, but please keep this to yourself. I don't want the whole office to know about this yet. And when and if I do, I want to be the one to tell them."

"Don't worry. My lips are sealed," Dennis assured me. The next thing I knew, he placed his hand on my shoulder. "Vanessa, if you're not a match, maybe I am. You can let that poor fellow, his sister, and everyone else involved know. As a matter of fact, you have my permission to give them my contact information when you go to the hospital today, or whenever you feel like it."

Anna whimpered. My eyes got as big as saucers. "Are you serious?" I asked.

"Of course! I'll admit I'm not as robust as I was ten years ago, but I'm still in pretty good health," Dennis said, patting his stomach. "My kidneys are in show-room condition."

"What about your family?" Anna asked.

"Pfffttt! You mean the son I only hear from when he needs money? Or the ex-wife who only communicates with me when the alimony checks are late? Other than a few cousins scattered here and there, this job is my real family."

"Dennis, are you serious about getting tested?" I asked.

"I'm as serious as a kidney transplant," he replied with a nervous laugh. This was the first time I'd ever seen so much sympathy displayed on his face.

I was so elated, I lost my appetite and couldn't finish my burrito. I hadn't even touched my diet Coke. When I returned to my desk and checked my cell phone for messages, I saw that Judith had called. She asked if I could leave work early so we could go to the hospital around four p.m.

I didn't waste any time trotting into Jim's office. He

raised his eyebrows when I shut the door and dropped down in one of the two seats in front of his desk.

"Uh-oh," he muttered. "You're scaring me."

I shook my head. "Don't worry. It's nothing for you to be scared about. Do you mind if I leave early today?"

Jim gave me a mock-annoyed look and hunched his shoulders. "No, I don't mind. May I ask why you need to leave?"

I spent the next ten minutes telling him the whole story. When I finished, he reared back in his chair and cupped his hands. "Vanessa, you're a brave young woman. I am behind you all the way. How much time will you need to take off for the surgery, if your kidney is suitable?"

"I'm not sure yet. But I have more than six and a half weeks' vacation accrued. And I have twice as much sick leave on the books."

Jim nodded and gave me a pensive look. "You do what you have to do and don't worry about work. If you need more time off, that won't be a problem. So long as you promise you'll come back."

I was thrilled to pieces that he was as supportive as Anna and Dennis. If my siblings and the rest of the people I had to tell weren't, I wouldn't be too upset.

"I'll call the temp agency and see if that same woman who filled in for me when I went to Hawaii last year will be available on the dates I need to take off. That is, *if* I need to take off. I may not even be a match."

"Let's hope you are. Good luck to you," Jim said. And then he did something he'd *never* done before: he gave me a big hug.

CHAPTER 15

When I met up with Judith Monday evening, we went to South Bay City General Hospital in my car. It was a short ride from her place, so we didn't have a lot of time to talk. "Vanessa, I can't tell you how much I appreciate what you're doing," she said with her voice trembling. "I can't wait to see Ronald's face when you tell him."

I was glad Odette was not on duty so I wouldn't have to explain anything to her yet. I still needed a little more time to digest what I was about to do.

Ronald was asleep when we got to his room. But the minute Judith touched his cheek, he opened his eyes. He blinked at her and then he gave me a curious look. "Hello, ladies," he wheezed.

"Baby brother, have I got news for you!" Judith hollered with her chest puffed out. "You remember Vanessa Hayes, don't you?

He nodded. "The passport lady." I was surprised to hear him laugh. Or that he was even able to laugh.

"Vanessa and I have had a few conversations since the day she came to visit, and she's made a very important decision. I'll let her tell you." Judith turned to me and nodded. When I didn't say anything, she gently nudged me with her elbow. "Tell him."

I sniffed and cleared my throat. My heart was thumping so hard and loud, I didn't get too close to the bed because I didn't want Ronald to hear it. "Um . . . I'm going to get tested to see if I can help you," I blurted out. Even if things didn't go the way I hoped they would, it warmed my heart tremendously just to see the way he immediately perked up.

Ronald's body jerked and his eyes widened. He glanced at Judith first with a puzzled expression on his face. And then he looked up at me, appearing more puzzled than before. "I don't know what to say. Thank you, Miss Hayes." His voice sounded much stronger now.

"Please call me Vanessa," I said with a forced grin.

"Please call me Ronald," he replied. He shifted his eyes from me to Judith and back. "When did you decide?"

"Last night. I had a long talk with my mother, and she said something that really got to me." I sniffed and cleared my throat. And then I told them about

Mama's situation. By the time I finished, Judith was almost in tears.

Ronald was so quiet and still, he looked like a cardboard figure. "What does your family have to say about you doing this for me?" he asked.

"My parents have some concerns, but they're okay with it. I haven't told anyone else yet. Well, a few people I work with know. But that's it."

"Vanessa, I don't know what to say," Ronald said with his voice faltering.

"You don't have to say anything. What's important is that I want to help you."

We visited with Ronald for a few minutes more. And would have stayed longer if I hadn't had to meet with his doctor in ten minutes.

Dr. Thomas was a heavyset man of medium height with thick, white hair and a jowly, red face. If he'd had a white beard and a red suit, he could have passed for Santa Claus's twin. He introduced himself, shook my hand, and waved me to a chair in front of his desk. He looked so serious, I scooted to the edge of my seat and listened with my stomach churning as he proceeded to rattle off information related to the procedures I would have to undergo. I was surprised, to say the least, because there was so much. To start, I'd have to submit to a psychological evaluation. And then, in addition to a basic medical screening, there was a long list of tests I'd have to endure—everything from cancer screening to a chest X-ray. Dr. Thomas disclosed a few other things that only confused me. I didn't tell him I was confused because I didn't want him to get the impression that I had made my decision on a lark. I figured that once we got things started, if I was still confused, I could get more clarification then. The main thing was, I didn't want him to not take me seriously and ultimately dismiss me as a potential donor. Dr. Thomas smiled for the first time since I'd entered his office. "Do you still want to go through with this, Ms. Hayes?"

Even though my heart was pounding and my head was throbbing, I was as determined as ever. But I wanted to get it over and done with as soon as possible. "Yes, I do. Can I get tested this week?"

"I'm sure we can get it started. What day works best for you?"

"Any day this week."

"Tomorrow's not good. This Wednesday is the earliest we can get you situated. There's a lot of paperwork, so you need to be back in my office Wednesday morning by eight a.m. The earlier in the day we start, the sooner we can get everything taken care of."

Dr. Thomas explained that if the folks in the lab were not too swamped, most of the tests could be administered on Wednesday. I cringed when he told me that all female donors had to undergo a gynecological exam and a mammogram. That couldn't be done until Thursday.

I left the hospital in a mild daze.

During the ride home, Judith kept telling me how much I had already changed Ronald's outlook. I didn't see any point in reminding her that I might not be a match. My biggest fear was, how hard would the results of my tests impact her and Ronald if they were negative? With all the other things on my mind, I pushed that thought to the back and hoped it would stay there until it was no longer an issue.

After I dropped Judith off at her apartment, I drove slowly toward my street, even though traffic was very light. I was glad that the dusky evening skyline in my rearview mirror looked so serene. It had a calming effect on me, which was something I needed more than ever because Dr. Thomas's words were still ringing in my ears. By the time I entered my apartment, I was in a fog of anticipation. One question that stood out in my mind was: *What have I gotten myself into?* But each time I thought about how much this situation was impacting Judith, not to mention Ronald, I told myself that no matter what, I would never back out.

I didn't just look tired, I felt like I had not gotten any sleep or rest in days. I stretched out on my couch and didn't wake up until almost eight a.m., Tuesday morning. I had just enough time to take a shower and get dressed for work. I hadn't eaten dinner the night before and my stomach was growling, so I picked up a snack at Starbucks on my way to the office.

Jim was okay with me taking off Wednesday and told me I should have taken off today as well so I could get plenty of rest before I checked into the hospital. Since I was already at the office, I decided to stay. I was glad I hadn't had to cancel the plans I'd made for tonight. But the last thing I wanted to do now was go on a date, even with Homer. I was glad I didn't cancel, though. Even if I didn't have a good time, at least it would take my mind off the series of compatibility tests I had coming up.

When I arrived at Dino's a few minutes before seven p.m., Madeline, Kirk, and Homer were already there—all dressed to kill. I wore the same green dress I'd worn on my last date with Barry. They had been seated at a table near the wall facing a life-size statue of a Roman gladiator.

Our waiter took our orders: huge plates of pasta and seafood for them and a chef's salad for me. The first few minutes were awkward; Kirk and Homer talked about sports and Madeline and I discussed her kids and our jobs. We all raved about the restaurant's spectacular Mediterranean decor and the soothing piped-in dinner music. I was thrilled when our orders finally came. And I was glad they had ordered champagne. I was feeling antsy, so it helped me relax.

"So, Vanessa, what have you been up to lately?" Homer asked with an amused look on his moon face. He had finished his meal and was now picking his teeth with a toothpick, which I thought was a crude thing for somebody to do in such an upscale restaurant. We had already listened to him describe his surgery in great detail.

"Just work and getting ready to do my Christmas shopping. I'm not looking forward to the crowds and the jacked-up prices," I said with a groan.

"That's why I always start in June. And I always save a ton of money," Homer said proudly. Then he started a lengthy complaint about the thirty-five pounds he'd gained because he hadn't been able to work out since his surgery. "My doctor had told me point blank that I wouldn't have to worry about losing or gaining weight. And just look at me, wearing a new suit big enough to cover a couch," he guffawed, and slapped his belly. "Humph! I've got a good mind to join Weight Watchers and send Dr. Brown the bill."

I was glad Madeline steered the conversation in another direction. "Vanessa, Homer had a problem with his mail last month, too," she stated. "The DMV lost his driver's license renewal application and he had to reapply." She smoothed down the sleeves of her hot-pink silk dress and gave me a wink.

"If that wasn't bad enough, when the DMV put the license in the mail, the post office lost it!" Kirk tossed in. His dreadlocks were slightly shorter than Madeline's. With his snazzy black suit and owlish features, he looked more like a professor than an IRS special agent who investigated potential criminal violations and related financial crimes.

"It's just as well. I'm still having some discomfort with my hip, so I won't be driving for a while anyway," Homer whined.

I remained silent while the three of them rambled on for ten minutes about subjects that didn't interest me much. All of a sudden, Kirk adjusted his tie, leaned back in his seat, and gave me a suspicious look. "V, you seem distracted. Is everything all right?"

"Huh? Oh! Everything is f-fine with me," I stammered. "It's just that today was one of those days at work. Things happened that I can't stop thinking about."

Homer gazed at me from the corner of his eye. "If you let whatever happens at work stay at work, you'd be better off. Take my word for it, V," he advised.

I didn't know how to respond to that, so I kept quiet. I did nod, though.

Madeline cleared her throat and glanced around the table, smiling at each face. "It's still early. Why don't we swing by the Spiderweb Club for a couple of hours?" she chirped. "I hear they've expanded the dance floor."

"It sounds like fun, but I'll have to pass tonight," I said quickly. "I have a few chores to take care of when I get home."

"I'd love to go to the club and get loose. It would help me jump-start my weight loss. But my hip is still a little too tender. Sometimes I can barely move without pain shooting up and down," Homer whimpered as he squirmed in his seat. And then he lifted my hand and gave it a quick peck. "Vanessa, I'm glad you were able to join us."

"I'm glad I was, too," I mumbled. "I had a nice time." The champagne bottle was empty, but they ordered coffee and dessert, so I knew it would be a while before they were ready to leave. I glanced at my watch. "If it's okay with everybody, I'm going to leave now."

"I'll call you tomorrow," Madeline said. And then she gave me a sheepish look and gently kicked my foot under the table.

"Let's get together again soon," Kirk suggested. "If we start out earlier the next time, we can check out a club or two."

"Um . . . yeah," I mumbled.

"I'll walk you to your car," Homer volunteered, already wobbling up. I stood up, hugged Madeline and Kirk, thanked them for dinner, and followed Homer out the door. He draped his arm around my shoulder and kept it there until we reached my two-year-old Toyota in the parking lot. He opened my door for me and held my hand. "I would have told you more about my surgery, but I could tell that Madeline and Kirk didn't want to hear any more about it," he said as he gazed into my eyes. I thought that was an odd thing for him to say, but I didn't comment.

When he sucked in some air and let go of my hand, I thought he was going to kiss me, but he didn't. Instead, he gave me a pat on the shoulder, spun around, and started trotting back to the restaurant so fast you would have thought a dog was chasing him. I was flabbergasted.

I was even more dumbfounded when I got home and saw the e-mail he had already sent me. **V, I really enjoyed your company tonight. But to be honest with you, I detected a little negative energy coming from you. Therefore, I don't think we should go any further. I might give you a call in a few weeks to let you know how I feel then.**

The date hadn't been much fun for me, but I didn't blame Homer. However, to be cordial, I decided to send him a reply and apologize for my "negative energy" and thank him for inviting me out. I was even more dumbfounded when I realized he had blocked me!

It was just as well. Under the circumstances, this was not the time for me to pursue a relationship with another man anyway. I was about to do something that might alter my life forever, and that was a lot more important for me to focus on.

CHAPTER 16

Judith gave me a wake-up call at six a.m., Wednesday morning, but I had already been up for an hour. She picked me up twenty minutes later to drive me to the hospital. "I hope you got a lot of rest last night," she said.

"I did. I had a dinner date, but I left the restaurant early."

Judith briefly glanced at me with a puzzled look on her face. "Oh? With someone interesting I hope."

"He's an interesting man all right." Judith howled when I gave her the lowdown on Homer, especially the part about the e-mail he sent me.

"I hope your next date turns out a lot better. I'm so glad I got married young. Even though there are some nice men out there, I would hate to get back into the dating scene. Have you considered any of those Internet dating sites?"

"Not yet. I know that it works for a lot of people.

But I'm still a little too skittish because of all the stories I've heard about catfishing and other deceptions."

Judith was going to spend time with Ronald while I was undergoing the test procedures, which would be performed at a clinic two blocks from the hospital. After that, she was going to go have lunch, do some shopping, and then wait for me to call her to pick me up and drive me back to my apartment.

I couldn't believe how many documents I had to sign and how many different tests were involved. They didn't do the last one for the day until six hours after I'd checked in. Judith was close by when I called her, so she arrived in less than ten minutes.

After I finished the last two procedures on Thursday morning, I returned to Dr. Thomas's office. He greeted me with a wide grin and waved me to a seat. Various parts of my body were tender from all the pricking, poking, and prodding I'd endured. So, I was not too comfortable when I sat down, and I hoped the meeting wouldn't last long. The first question I asked was, "How long is it going to take to get the test results?"

"I'm sure we'll have some of them by next week. The rest could take up to two to three months. If you're compatible, the Human Tissue Authority has to okay the transplant. And then the entire transplant team has to be available to perform the surgery. I'm certain that we'll be able to proceed by April or March."

My heart sank. All this information overwhelmed me. I was glad I hadn't known so much was involved before I decided to become a donor. If I had, I wasn't sure I would have gone through with it after all. I was grateful things turned out this way because now I couldn't back out if I wanted to—and I didn't. "Four months is so far away." I gulped and gave Dr. Thomas a hopeful look. "Please tell me that Ronald can hang on for that long."

"I wish I could. All we can hope for is the best. But we have to be prepared for the worst."

Now that I knew I would have to wait a while to get the results, I didn't want to put off telling my siblings and Madeline and Odette. I was going to need a lot of support to make it through the waiting period.

I left a voice mail for Jim and Anna to let them know I'd be returning to work tomorrow. I saw no reason to waste Friday at home when I didn't have to. Madeline answered on the third ring when I called her number. "It's about time you called me back. I left you a message Wednesday afternoon to see what you thought about Homer," she began. "He didn't mention you after he returned to the restaurant. Are things headed in the right direction for you two?"

"Things between Homer and me are headed to a dead end," I said sternly.

Madeline let out a sharp, short whimper when I told her about the e-mail he'd sent. "Did you reply? It would be nice if he'd given you a more detailed explanation. Especially after the way he kept after us to set him up with you."

"I tried to reply, but he'd already blocked me."

Madeline didn't whimper this time; she screamed. And then we laughed. When we stopped, I said, "I have to share something with you. It's about Ronald Guthrie."

"Isn't he the man who needs a kidney?"

"Uh-huh." I took a deep breath and told her everything. I even shared the part about Mama's transplant and how that had influenced my decision. When I stopped talking, she remained silent for so long, I wasn't sure she was still on the phone. "You still there?"

"I'm here. This is the biggest bombshell anybody ever dropped on me. I had to take a moment to let it sink in. How come you're just now sharing this? Have you told Odette?"

"No, but I'll tell her later."

"I don't know what to say, V!"

"You can say whatever you want. I'm in this too deeply now to change my mind and back out."

"I wouldn't want you to do that. But whatever you do, I'm behind you all the way."

I was happy that Madeline was on my side. She

spent the next few minutes commending me and telling me how much she admired my courage. It pleased me to know that so many of the people in my life supported my decision. After we ended our call, I called Odette. She didn't hesitate either to let me know what a wonderful and unselfish thing I was doing. "V, after everything is over, lets you and me and Madeline go away for a few days and celebrate."

"I'm all for that. We can discuss that later. Now I need to get in touch with Gary and Debra and let them know."

I got Gary's and Debra's voice mail. I told them they needed to return my call ASAP. I didn't want to tell my parents about the tests over the phone, so I drove to the retirement center. I was happy Debra and Gary were present when I got there.

After I greeted everybody and before I could sit down or say anything else, Debra started unloading a mouthful of words so fast I couldn't get one in edgewise. "I'm glad you're here, V. I was going to pay you a visit. You don't have to lend me money to pay a babysitter on Christmas Eve. The party is going to be at our house. More people are going to come than we thought, and Roger's apartment is too small. Anyway, I've been dying to show off our beautiful new home. If you change your mind about driving to Reno, you should come to the party. Besides, I don't know what you were thinking when you made your plans. You know how heavy the snow gets on the highway once you make it up into the mountains this time of year. Last year it was so bad, folks going to and coming from Reno got stranded for twelve hours."

I was glad when she finally paused. But the way her lips were parted, it looked like she'd stopped just to catch her breath and was gearing up to jabber some more. But I didn't let her. "I've already canceled Reno, but I don't think I'll feel like attending a big party." I looked from her to Gary. "I'm glad you're both here so I won't have to say this but once." Mama and Debra were on the couch, and I sat down on the arm close to Mama. She kept a straight face, but Debra's eyes were stretched open so wide, her eyeballs looked like they were trying to escape.

Daddy was lying across his bed in his pajamas. Gary was sitting at the foot of Mama's bed. He rubbed the back of his head and mouthed, "Oh Lord. I have a feeling this is something I don't want to hear."

I blew out a loud breath. "Mama and Daddy already know what I'm about to do, but it's time for me to tell you two now." My brother and sister sat as stiff as trees and as quiet as mice until I stopped talking.

"I can't believe my ears! *You're going to give up one of your kidneys?*" Debra shrieked. "W-why? You just met that woman and her brother last month!"

Gary stood up with his arms folded and stared at me as if I'd lost my mind. "Girl, they better be paying you some *big* bucks!" he barked.

"I'm not getting paid anything. Even if they offered me money, I wouldn't accept it," I declared.

"Why not? I read about some people who sold one of their kidneys for ten thousand dollars!" Debra boomed.

"I'm not 'some people' and I'm doing it because I want to. Ronald's insurance will cover all of my medical expenses and that's enough for me."

The room got so quiet, you could have heard a pin drop. Debra leaped up off the couch and put her hands on her hips. "Well, I don't like what you're doing! Do you think those people would do something like this for you?"

"What if something happens to your other kidney?" Gary asked with a seriously concerned look on his face.

"If that happens, I hope somebody will donate a new kidney to me," I replied. "The doctor told me that my remaining kidney will eventually increase in size to compensate for the loss of the other one."

"Yuck!" Debra scrunched up her lips and looked from Mama to Daddy. "Are you two just going to sit there? Say something to your child!" She was wagging her finger so hard, I was surprised it didn't fall off.

Mama raised her eyebrows and gently said, "I'm not about to stop her. It's her kidney."

"What's wrong with you, Mama? This is your firstborn child! Aren't you and Daddy going to try and talk some sense into her? I never thought this family would get caught up in an organ transplant situation!" Debra hollered.

Immediately after Debra's last sentence, Daddy sat up and turned to Mama with a look of defeat on his face. And then he said in a gentle tone, "Ocie, don't let this get out of hand. I think it's high time for you to tell Gary and Debra what you went through."

Debra and Gary whirled around to face Mama with their mouths hanging open.

Mama sighed and started talking in a slow, controlled manner. By the time she finished telling my siblings everything she'd told me about her liver transplant, Debra was in tears and Gary looked like he had turned to stone.

"Mama, how come you didn't tell us before now?" Gary wanted to know.

"Because it wasn't important until now," she replied.

Gary walked over to me and put his hands on my shoulders. "V, if you're a match and decide to go through with the transplant, you can stay with me until you recover." My brother rarely showed his emotions. This was the first time in years I'd seen tears in his eyes.

"No, Gary's only got one bedroom. You can either stay with us, or I'll come hang out at your place until you're back on your feet," Debra offered with her voice cracking.

"Thanks," I replied meekly. It was a struggle for me to hold back my tears.

A few moments of awkward silence passed. I let out a sigh of relief and stood up. I wanted to stay longer, but I was getting too emotional. "The test results won't all come in at the same time. But as they come in, I'll keep you all posted." After a long group hug, I immediately left.

CHAPTER 17

I knew that waiting for my test results was not going to be easy. I could barely eat, and each night I tossed and turned for hours when I went to bed. By the third day, I was climbing the walls. I wanted to make sure I was available whenever they called so I kept my cell phone close by.

When Anna approached my desk on Monday morning to see if we were having our weekly lunch at Juanita's, I gave her a weary look and shook my head. "I'd rather go to that salad bar on Spring Street. I might even skip lunch and spend a little time on the treadmill today if it's available."

"When has it not been available? You and I are the only two employees who take full advantage of having a fitness center on the premises. Do you have to lose a few pounds before the surgery?" Anna asked as she sat down on the corner of my desk.

"Dr. Thomas didn't tell me I had to lose weight, but I won't be able to eat the way I used to. He gave me a long list of foods and beverages I should avoid until after the surgery, though." Unfortunately, the list included items I'd taken for granted all my life and scarfed down like they were going out of style. I wouldn't miss the bacon, Big Macs, and pasta, but I was a fool for fried meat. I couldn't remember the last time I'd made it through a whole week without picking up a bucket of spicy fried chicken from KFC, or frying some of my own. "I can deal with it for a couple of weeks without going crazy. But he said it could take up to four months for all of test results to be ready."

"I wish this had happened earlier in the year. If it had, you'd still be able to enjoy a normal Christmas," Anna said, giving me a mournful look.

"It couldn't have happened at a better time. Christmas is the time for sharing and helping, and I'm giving the most important gift I'll ever give."

Anna gazed at me in awe. "That's a great attitude. I'm glad you feel that way. Just think about all the lives your good deed will impact."

"This is way more than a 'good deed.' It's an honor."

On my way home from work, I picked up a small

Christmas tree and spent an hour decorating it. I was pleased with the tinsel and bulbs for now, but I knew I'd be adding more items later. I also decorated my living-room window with blinking lights and a huge wreath. I had been making mental notes and collecting hints from people since October about what they wanted for Christmas. So, I had a lot of shopping to do.

Judith called me up a few minutes past nine p.m. She was excited because her husband had called from Afghanistan a few hours earlier. "Arthur was ecstatic when I told him about you. He can't wait to meet you. He's been telling me all along that we'd find a donor," she gushed.

"Um, Judith, maybe we shouldn't tell anybody else until we know for sure that I'm a match."

"You're right. But I've kept Arthur up to date about all the other people who got tested. I don't see any reason to be too closemouthed now. Besides, each time we get a potential donor, it lifts everybody's spirits, especially Ronald's. I spoke to my son, Paul, last night, too. He's coming home for Christmas and is also looking forward to meeting you."

"I'm flattered. But I feel like a standout. What about all the other folks who got tested?"

"They were either family members or friends. You're special. Ronald said so himself."

I smiled. "So is he," I said shyly.

Each time my phone rang at home and at work, my heart skipped a beat. I didn't have much of an appetite, so I spent part of my lunch hours on the office treadmill each day. I skipped Friday when Jim brought one of his wife's scrumptious fruit-cakes to the office. I scarfed down two slices during my morning break with Anna and Dennis in our break room. The table we shared was cluttered with crumbs, saucers, coffee cups, and soiled napkins.

"So, do you think this waiting game will be over by next week?" Anna asked, as she wiped crumbs off her lips.

"I had hoped it would be over this week," I replied. "But I'm not as jittery as I was the first few days."

"By the way, since you're not going to drive up to Reno for Christmas, what are you going to do for the holiday?" Dennis asked.

"Well, my sister is going to cook up a storm. She'll have a lot of company, and with all the things on my mind now, I don't want to be around a big crowd. I might cook a little something and watch all my favorite holiday movies."

"Why don't you come to my house?" Anna invited.

"It's only going to be Gus, myself, and a few relatives."

"You haven't been to my place in a while. I'd love for you to join my lady friend and me, my son, and a couple of neighbors," Dennis threw in.

"Thanks to both of you, but I'd rather stay home," I insisted. "Let's wait and do something after this is all over."

Before I knew it, it was the week before Christmas. I finished my shopping that Friday evening. I almost filled the trunk of my car, the backseat, and the passenger seat with packages and shopping bags. After I left the mall, I treated myself to a facial at a spa I frequently visited. I felt so relaxed after that, I took the long route home so I could gaze at some of the decorations in our business district. The sights were spectacular, colorful blinking lights everywhere, excessively decorated trees, and even a few life-size reindeer. It was the same in the residential areas. The most awesome display was a ten-foot-tall fake snowman on the front lawn of a large apartment building a block from mine.

When I got home, I returned calls to Mama and Madeline before I broiled a few pieces of chicken, made a salad, and watched *How the Grinch Stole Christmas* for the umpteenth time.

The long wait for my test results finally ended three days before Christmas. I had been home from work for only five minutes that Monday when my phone rang. It was Dr. Thomas.

"Ms. Hayes, I have great news! You are a perfect match."

CHAPTER 18

It took a few seconds for Dr. Thomas's words to sink in. When they did, I asked one of the most boneheaded questions I'd ever asked. "Are you sure?"

"I'm sure," he chuckled. He spent the next couple of minutes going over some of the same details we'd already discussed.

When he asked if I had any more questions, I said something almost as silly as my first question. "Will having only one kidney impact my ability to have a normal sex life and conceive children when I get married?"

My question must have caught him off guard because he didn't answer right away. "Oh! Trust me, you'll be able to do everything you do now. I thought I'd already made that clear."

"I'm sure you did. But there is so much to remember, I guess I forgot that part."

He made a few more remarks before he hung up.

When I put the phone down and stood up from the couch, I felt light-headed. Knowing that I was a match put a different spin on things. Up until now, giving up one of my kidneys had only been a possibility. Now it was a reality. I was about to give away a part of my body that I could never get back.

Judith didn't answer her phone when I called her, so I spent the next hour calling everybody else I knew to share my good news. "Well, I'll have to cancel the cruise your daddy and me were going to go on tomorrow," Mama told me.

"You'll do no such thing. Before they do the surgery, the final approval has to come from the Human Tissue Authority and the entire transplant team has to be available. Dr. Thomas said the surgery will take place either in April or March. There is no reason for you and Daddy to cancel your cruise."

"Baby, we don't want you to be alone on the holiday with a surgery hanging over your head!" Mama boomed. "We can always go on a cruise."

"Then go this time. If you cancel this close to the departure date, you'll lose all of your money. Besides, if I decide to do something else on Christmas Day, two of my coworkers invited me to have dinner with them."

It was only a few minutes past six-thirty p.m. and I was so antsy I had to get out of the house. Without giving it a second thought, I decided to visit Ronald.

He looked extremely excited to see me. "You're a sight for sore eyes! I was just thinking about you. Dr. Thomas told me the great news about the results of your tests. I planned to give you a call tomorrow," he said as he struggled to sit up. I stopped by the side of his bed and gently took his hand in mine. I was amazed at how warm he felt.

"I can't tell you how happy I was when he called me. I'm sorry to be coming here so late, but I had to," I said.

"Vanessa, it's never too late for you to come see me. Visiting hours at this hospital are twenty-four hours per day."

"I know, but I still didn't want to come so late. I drove at breakneck speed to get here before it got any later. I wish I had decided to come before I got on the phone and started calling people to let them know. I've been over the moon since Dr. Thomas called me up this evening." I was feeling so giddy I couldn't stop grinning and holding his hand. In an awed tone, I continued. "If I had received my passport in time, I'd be in Paris at this very moment."

Ronald gave me a tight smile and a weak nod. What he said next caught me so off guard, my knees almost buckled. "Your first trip to Paris will be on me. First class all the way."

My breath caught in my throat and I blinked at him a few times. I could feel sweat oozing from my body, so I moved my hand away from his. I didn't care if he was serious or not; his offer made my day. I was so elated, I wanted to dance a jig. I managed to remain composed. "I'm going to hold you to that." I laughed and I was glad he did, too.

Ronald sat up straighter and gave me a pensive look. "Vanessa, I know I've already thanked you, but I want to thank you again."

I was about to hold his hand again when I heard a commotion behind me. When I whirled around, I was glad to see Judith, but shocked and—I had to admit, though I didn't know why—disappointed to see Jan with her.

"Vanessa, I'm so glad to see you!" Judith hollered. "Dr. Thomas told me the wonderful news. I left you a message a little while ago." She scurried over to me and gave me a hug. When she released me, she exhaled and beckoned to Jan to come closer. "Jan, this is Vanessa Hayes, the beautiful woman I told you about."

"I am so happy to meet you!" Jan squealed. She grabbed my hand and shook it so hard my arm ached. "I've heard so much about you!"

"I'm happy to finally meet you, too," I managed. "So, you're Ronald's friend." I couldn't bring myself to say fiancée because I had no idea what the status of their relationship was now. She didn't waste any time clearing that up.

"Actually, I'm his fiancée," she declared, with what looked like a smirk on her face.

"Oh yeah," I mumbled.

When I saw that Ronald looked even happier, I felt better about Jan's appearance. She abruptly turned from me and hovered over his bed, smoothing his hair back with her hand. "Honey, I was ecstatic when I heard the news that they'd finally found a match!" Just as abruptly, she turned her attention back to me. "I hope you don't change your mind."

I thought that was an airheaded comment for her to make after all I'd been through. "Change my mind? Why would I do that?"

"Well, my understanding is that they won't do the surgery until sometime next year. A lot can happen between now and then. Are you married or do you have a significant other? What if your relatives talk you out of going through with it?"

"You don't have to worry. Nobody is going to talk me out of anything," I said firmly.

Jan gave me a guarded look, but she didn't say anything else on the subject. She hovered over Ronald even more and started caressing the side of his face. "Now we can still enjoy Christmas like we planned. I'm going to prepare a feast and bring you a nice plate. Paul will be home from school and he'll be joining Judith at my house with my family."

"I hope Vanessa will join us, too," Judith tossed in.

I was surprised, but I managed not to show it. "How about it, Vanessa?"

I responded very casually, "I'm sorry, but I've already made other plans."

"That's a shame," Jan said with a tight look on her face.

"I hope you'll have a very merry Christmas, Vanessa," Ronald told me. "It's a shame we can't all celebrate it together."

"I promise I'll come by at some point on Christmas Day, Ronald," I said. "If I can't make it, I'll give you a call."

His eyes lit up. "That would be so nice. I'll be looking forward to it." From the corner of my eye, I saw that Jan's face looked even tighter.

CHAPTER 19

Jim closed the office at noon on Christmas Eve every year. But only five or six people showed up on this day anyway. Today, it was three of the folks in the personnel office, Anna, and myself. After she and I exchanged gifts fifteen minutes past ten a.m., she decided to leave for the day.

We shared our floor with a small printing company, but they had shut down for the whole week. The folks in the personnel office left one by one, a few minutes apart. By ten-thirty, I was the only person on the premises. I took off five minutes later so I could drop off the gifts in the trunk of my car to Debra, Gary, and a couple of church members. Madeline, Odette, and I had stopped exchanging gifts several years ago. Up until then, I had always given presents to them, their spouses, and their kids. Not to mention other relatives and some of my neighbors. But when it finally got to be too much, I stopped. Besides, I did enough for everybody during the year.

Debra woke me up with a phone call right after dawn on Christmas morning. "V, I know you don't plan on sitting in that apartment all by yourself today. The least you can do is come have dinner with us."

I was so groggy, I had to slap the side of my head to get my bearings. "I might. But I think I'll run over to the hospital and pay Ronald a visit first. I told him that I would give him a call today, but I'd rather see him in person."

"What time are you going?"

"I thought I'd do it early in the day. Hopefully before noon. Why?"

"I can't wait to meet this man. Pick me up so I can go with you. Stephen can keep an eye on the turkey and the kids. Our guests won't arrive until this evening."

"Wouldn't you rather wait and meet him after the surgery?"

"No, I want to meet this mystery man now. And it's about time."

I didn't want to argue with my sister, so I agreed to pick her up.

Unfortunately, when we got to the hospital, a stern-faced nurse intercepted us before we could enter Ronald's room and told us he was not up to having company. "But I'm his donor," I explained.

"It doesn't matter. The doctor says no visits, period. His sister and fiancée came a little while ago and I couldn't let them in either."

Debra and I left. Before we made it to the elevators, she put her arm around my shoulder. "Sis, what if he doesn't live long enough to have the transplant?"

I shuddered so hard, I almost fell. "Please don't say that. Don't even think it!" I snapped. "He *has* to live long enough. . . ."

When Debra and I got to her house, she tried to talk me into staying for dinner. But, knowing that Ronald was not doing well, I was feeling pretty downhearted. All I wanted to do was go back home. I did go in to say hello to Stephen and the kids and to check out all the new decorations Debra had purchased since my last visit. The food was ready, so I fixed a huge plate to take home.

I called Judith the minute I got in my door. She had just come home from Jan's house. After she told me in great detail about the wonderful meal Jan had served, I told her, "I tried to visit Ronald a little while ago, but the nurse wouldn't let me in his room. What's going on?"

"Nothing to worry about. It's just that he didn't sleep at all last night, so he was pretty exhausted this morning. They're just being cautious." Judith cleared her throat. "My son arrived last night. Would you like to come over and meet him?"

"Um, no. I didn't get much sleep myself last night, so I'm going to just rest."

"I understand. Well, do you want me to bring you a plate? Jan let us take enough food to feed an army. I'll bring Paul with me so he can finally meet you. He's only going to stay until Saturday. He's going to be running around with his friends, and I'm sure you'll be busy with your family, so he might not get to meet you otherwise."

"You don't have to bring any food. My sister fixed me a huge plate. But why don't you and your son come over?"

They arrived an hour later. Paul was a younger version of Ronald and just as charming. After the introduction, I waved him and Judith to my couch. They declined the coffee I offered. I sat in the wing chair facing them. I could tell from the way Paul was blinking and fidgeting that he was nervous. He'd said very little so far. Then all of a sudden, he cleared his throat and words started flying out of his mouth like birds. "Miss Vanessa, you don't know how happy I am that my mama and Uncle Ron met you! He can't stop talking about you," he said with his voice cracking. "I thought that this was going to be the worst Christmas our family ever had, but you changed all that."

Such a display of emotion startled me, especially coming from such a young man. "I'm so glad I am able to help." It was a struggle for me to hold back my tears. I didn't want to get too emotional myself, so I abruptly changed the subject. "How are things at school, Paul?"

"Okay, I guess," he replied as he rolled his eyes. I was glad he looked more relaxed now. "I'll be glad when I graduate, though. I'm thinking about staying on in DC and pursuing a few opportunities."

Judith gently slapped his arm. "We have just as many jobs for engineers out here, maybe even more." She snickered and gave me a weary look. "One of the opportunities he's thinking about pursuing is named Gail. . . ."

"My brother Gary is still pursuing those same kind of 'opportunities,'" I said.

Paul liked to talk, so he dominated the conversation. He raved about everything from his cool professors, to music, and to Gail. I was glad when he asked for my permission to go into the kitchen to check his messages and return some calls.

"You can go to my bedroom down the hall and

shut the door," I suggested. "That way you can have more privacy."

"Okay!" He gave me a wide-eyed grin and sprinted out of the room.

"Judith, thanks for coming over." I shifted in my seat and blinked at her. "Uh, I've been meaning to tell you, I'm glad Jan reconsidered her decision."

There was a doubtful look on Judith's face, but she nodded. "I am too, but I'm not getting my hopes up too high. Even after the surgery, Ronald may need a lot of care for quite a while. There is a chance that he may have other issues later. Dr. Thomas assured him that he'd be able to function as normally as any other healthy man. The doctor could be right, and he could not be right. My main concern is that Ronald might never be able to have a full relationship with a woman, which would mean . . . no children. I *know* Jan wouldn't be able to accept that."

"I hope it doesn't come to that. Will he continue to stay with you when they release him?"

"For the first week or two. His recovery period could be anywhere from two to twelve weeks. I have to return to work by the end of February, so if he needs full-time care, I'll hire a nurse." Judith let out a loud, weary sigh. "I don't know if Jan will be able to hang in there that long."

"Everything is going to be just fine. That's what's important, so let's focus on that." I told Ronald about Judith's visit and what a wonderful impression his nephew had made on me.

"Paul's a great kid. I hope to have one like him someday. . . ."

"You will." An awkward moment of silence passed. "I don't want to keep you from getting your rest, so I'll let you go for now. I'll call again soon."

"Judith gave me your cell phone number. Do you mind if I call you up from time to time? Since I'm going to be laid up for God knows how long, I'd like to have something interesting to look forward to."

"You can call me up as often as you want. I'd like that very much." I held my breath for a couple of seconds before I told him, "In case you can't reach me on my cell, I'll give you my landline and work phone numbers, too."

"Thank you. You have no idea how much that means to me."

Ronald's last comment, and the mysterious tone of his voice, made my heart feel like it was about to turn upside down. My face got so hot I had to fan it. No other man had ever affected me this way. For the first time, I realized I wanted to be more to him than just a friend and kidney donor. However, despite how nice

"If she was willing to resume the relationsh
she knows all the facts, why wouldn't she?"

Judith looked at me like I was crazy. "If she
hang in there the first time, how do we know
able to do it this time?"

"Let's give her the benefit of the doubt."
force myself to sound optimistic. "I'm sure sl
loves Ronald. And, this whole episode jus
make their love even stronger."

As much as I was enjoying Judith and Paul
was glad when they left an hour later. I need
time alone to reflect on everything that w
pening.

Knowing that Ronald wasn't feeling too w
cided it probably wouldn't be a good idea to
But because I had told him I would—and I
me he'd be looking forward to it—I called
phone. If he didn't answer, I could at leas
voice mail, so he'd know that I'd kept my pr
was a good thing I did call.

He answered on the first ring. "Vanessa!
most given up on you!" His voice was so l
strong, I assumed he was doing much better

"I tried to visit you today," I said meekly.

"I heard. I'm sorry about that. I'm also s
things are moving so slowly. If I'm on pins
dles, I can't imagine how you must be feeling

he was to me, I didn't want to presume anything about how he felt about me. And I was not about to initiate anything more serious and risk being disappointed or embarrassed. I planned to leave everything up to him.

CHAPTER 20

I spent New Year's Eve with Mama and Daddy. The retirement home hosted a party in the recreation room and invited the residents' family members. They had party hats and noisemakers, a three-piece band, and plenty of food and champagne. I was the youngest nonresident in attendance. All the other residents' relatives were in their late forties and fifties. But that didn't bother me. I had made a lot of new elderly friends at the home. But when a married couple in their nineties kept asking me why a "young girl" like me wasn't at a nightclub or party with people my age, I decided it was time to go.

I escorted my parents back to their room. We set our party hats on the coffee table. While Mama was in the bathroom, Daddy plopped down next to me on the couch and asked, "What's going to happen after that transplant deal is over?"

"Ronald will live a long, normal life, I hope."

"That's not what I meant. I don't even know the man and I feel for him, but I'm more interested in what it's going to mean to you. Are you going to spend a lot of time with him and his sister?"

"I hope so. I don't know what all is going to happen. But Ronald and I will be bonded for life, so it would be nice to stay in touch with him. And I like Judith and her son, so I'd like to get to know them better, as well as the rest of that family."

"I'm glad you feel that way," Daddy said.

"What way, Alex?" Mama asked as she shuffled back into the room. She sat down on the side of her bed, rubbing lotion onto her arms.

"Vanessa is planning to get real close to that man and his whole family after the operation."

Mama set her lotion on her nightstand and gave Daddy a curious look. "Do you have a problem with that? I've heard that a lot of recipients develop long-term relationships with their donors." Mama gazed at me with her eyes narrowed. "Didn't you tell us that Ronald's fiancée came back into the picture?"

"Yes, she did," I muttered. "They'll get married eventually."

"Humph. He'd better think twice about counting on her to stick around," Mama snapped.

"Mama, don't be too harsh. The woman is only human," I defended.

"Exactly. If she ran once, she could run again," she insisted.

Daddy had more to say on the subject. "You can be friends with that man, but I advise you not to get too close. Especially if he marries that other woman. The last thing you want to do is be a thorn in some woman's side because of her husband."

I shook my head and heaved out an exasperated sigh. I didn't know what to say about Daddy's last comment, so I decided it was time to leave.

When I got up on New Year's Day and returned calls to Madeline and Odette, they couldn't stop laughing when I told them how most of the retirement home residents had fallen asleep before the New Year arrived. I laughed, even though I didn't think it was funny. Old age was one thing we'd all experience, if we were lucky.

All I wanted was for everybody I cared about to be as happy as I was.

The third week in January, Anna announced that she was finally pregnant with her first child. "I was beginning to think it was never going to happen," she gushed to me in the ladies' room that Monday morning.

"I'm so happy for you," I said, giving her a bear hug. "You'll be a great mother."

She shared the news with the rest of our coworkers

during our weekly staff meeting an hour later. Out of nowhere, Dennis yelled across the room, "Vanessa, when are you going to get married and start a family? You're the only singleton left at the company!"

"Uh-uh. Pablo in the mail room is still single," one of the engineers hollered.

"My cousin is available, but I don't think he's Vanessa's type," another one hollered.

I laughed along with everybody else, but I didn't like being teased or singled out. I never complained about it; however, the fact that I was now the only employee at the company who had never been married or had any children saddened me. I didn't stay sad long, though. Even if Mama hadn't kept telling me that "everything happens for a reason" and that I was going to receive my rewards someday, I was still happy with my life. But in the back of my mind, I hoped that Mama's predictions would come true.

The weeks dragged on and the next thing I knew, it was March. Ronald's condition was no worse, but from the conversations I had with him, he was so optimistic, he had already started planning the rest of his life. He mentioned everything from buying a new car to adding another room to his house. To my surprise, he said nothing about marrying Jan.

Tuesday morning before I even left for work, my phone rang. My heart skipped a beat when I heard

Dr. Thomas's voice. "Ms. Hayes, I have some very good news. We'll be doing Mr. Guthrie's surgery this week."

I was so ecstatic I could barely speak. "I am so happy to hear that! What day this week?"

"I hope you're not superstitious because we have you scheduled to check into the clinic this Friday, which also happens to be the thirteenth. I hope the date works for you. If it doesn't, the transplant team won't be available again until later in the month."

"That date is fine with me!" I hollered. "I don't want to put this off another day."

Dr. Thomas said a few other things, some he had already repeated more than once. But I was so anxious for him to get off the phone, I could barely contain myself. When he finally did, the first person I called was Ronald. I got his cell phone voice mail, so I called Odette. She was as excited as I was about the upcoming surgery on Friday. "Ronald is very happy. He had to have some more blood work done, so he won't be back in his room for a while. Why don't you give him a call in a couple of hours?"

"Blood work? I thought they had done everything that needed to be done before the surgery."

"Don't panic, V. He's fine. This happens all the time. I'm surprised they haven't had you come in for more tests."

"Please don't say that. They had me come in for another urine sample and another X-ray last month."

"I know all about that. Now you get some rest the next few days. You're going to need it."

I called up everybody else I could think of. They were just as excited as I was.

When I got to work Tuesday morning, Jim told me to go back home and not come back until after everything was over. "You'll be less of a woman, but that won't bother me," he teased. When I realized what he meant, I laughed with him. "Vanessa, you won't regret what you're doing, and I am confident everything will work out for you and the recipient, whatever his name is."

"His name is Ronald," I said proudly. "And he's not just 'the recipient,' he's my friend."

CHAPTER 21

I only slept for about three hours Thursday night. But when I got up Friday morning at six a.m. I was not the least bit tired or sleepy.

Judith picked me up an hour later and drove me to the transplant clinic, which was where the procedures would be performed. The surgery would take only a few hours, but I'd be able to go home in two or three days, and return to my normal routine in three to six weeks. Ronald's recovery could take twice as long.

I was glad Judith interrupted the thoughts swimming around in my head. "Vanessa, for the first time since this all started, I think my brother is really scared." She sounded scared herself, and so was I.

"The good thing is, he's got so much support. I don't think he'll be scared for long. Especially after the surgery is over. I'm sure having Jan back in his life is a big help."

Judith glanced at me. I was surprised to see a mysterious smile on her face. "Uh-uh. She's out of the picture."

"Again?" I hollered. "This is the second time."

Judith shook her head and said with her voice quivering, "She didn't end it this time, he did."

I was surprised and pleased to hear this new development. From the little I knew about Jan, I had come to the conclusion that she was not the right woman for a man like Ronald. He deserved better and I planned to pray that he would find a suitable mate. In the meantime, I didn't want Judith to think that I was remotely interested in her brother's romantic relationships, so I had to say something neutral. I groped for the best response I could come up with: "That's too bad."

Judith began to speak in a more serious tone. "I keep my nose out of his personal business when it involves women. I was tempted to let him know what I thought after the cold way she walked away from him the first time. But when he told me yesterday that he'd broken off things with her permanently, I told him how thrilled I was to hear that. At the end of the day, he's a grown man and knows what he wants. And he's very intelligent. So, when the right woman comes along, he'll know it."

"I'm sure he will," I mumbled.

Even though Odette would be the attending nurse during the surgery, I was still nervous. The last thing I remembered after I'd been prepped was her telling me, "We're all praying, so you don't have anything to worry about. Besides, you'll be in the hands of some of the state's best surgeons."

The next thing I knew, I was opening my eyes in a recovery room. I was glad to see Odette's smiling face. "You did good, girl," she commented with a wink.

I was groggy and my throat felt so dry, I couldn't get any words out. All I could do was nod and that took a lot of effort. I closed my eyes again and the next time I opened them, it was dark outside. This time it was Dr. Thomas hovering over me. "How do you feel?" he asked in a low tone with a sympathetic look on his face.

Before I answered, I sat up and looked around. I was now in a different room. "All right, I guess. How is Ronald?" I croaked.

"He's in another recovery room and he's doing incredibly well."

I lifted the covers and gently slid my hand over my lower midsection. I scrunched up my face and winced from the pain, which wasn't as bad as I thought it would be. I shifted my body a little and the soreness seemed more intense, so I decided to lie as still as I could. "How long will I be sore and how long will I have to wear this bandage?" I asked with a grimace.

"The soreness will go away in about a week, maybe

even sooner. But you'll have to wear the bandage until the incision is fully healed to avoid infection. And don't worry about the bloating. That'll all be gone before you know it."

"H-how come nobody's been to see me?"

Dr. Thomas gave me an incredulous look. "Are you kidding? Next to Mr. Guthrie, you're the most popular patient we have right now. Your parents, your siblings, a few friends, your boss, and a few of your other coworkers came by earlier today. Don't you remember?"

"No. I must have really been out of it, huh?"

"Apparently. But I'm sure they will all return or call before you leave."

When I woke up on the second day, I almost felt like my old self. The same folks, Dr. Thomas had told me, who'd come by the first day all came back. I had so many flowers and cards, they had to bring in an extra stand to set them on. Judith didn't arrive until half past noon after everybody else had left. She set a potted plant and a card on the stand before she skittered over and kissed my sweaty forehead. "Vanessa, you've given my family a new lease on life and we will all be forever grateful," she gushed.

"Thank you," I mumbled. "How is Ronald doing today?"

"He's doing just great!" she exclaimed with a dreamy-eyed look on her face. "He's had a lot of company today and he's a little worn out. But he's been asking about you. And, I have a gift for you from him." Judith opened her large purse and pulled out a box wrapped in silver paper and handed it to me. It was the size of a book, so that's what I assumed it was. "I'm sure you'll like it."

I was puzzled and eager to see what was inside. "Should I open it now?"

"Why not? There is no reason for you to wait."

I gently removed the wrapping and opened the box. It contained an eight-inch-tall bronze replica of the Eiffel Tower with the words *We're waiting for you, Vanessa* engraved at the bottom. A smile spread across my face. "Where did he get this?"

"He had one of our cousins in London pick it up on his recent holiday in Paris."

"This is so nice," I managed as I admired my gift. I was so touched by Ronald's thoughtful gesture, I had to hold my breath to keep from crying. And I had to blink hard to hold back my tears. "When will he be well enough for me to visit his room?"

"I'll check with his nurse. You're probably the one person he wants to see most of all."

An hour after Judith left, someone knocked on my door. Before I could respond, the door eased open and Odette pushed a wheelchair into the room with Ronald in it. She parked him by the side of my bed. As soon as I saw the condition of his face, I widened my eyes and gulped. I hoped he felt better than he looked. It looked like most of the blood had drained out of his face. His skin was so dry it looked like sandpaper. "I'll leave you two alone for a few minutes." Odette smiled and gave me a thumbs-up before she scurried out.

Ronald's hand was shaking, but he still managed to reach over and wrap it around mine. "Thank you again, Vanessa. You've given me the gift of life and I will be eternally grateful." He sounded strong, despite how weak he looked. "No matter where you or I go, we will always be connected." He chuckled and gently tapped his midsection.

"You don't have to keep thanking me." I picked up the cute gift I'd received from him off my nightstand and held it in front of his face. "And you didn't have to do this. I'm glad you did, though. I love it."

"I'm sorry I didn't think to do it weeks ago." Ronald didn't sound so strong now. His voice had dropped almost to a whisper.

I got worried when he started coughing. "Do you want me to call for the nurse?"

"Y-yes," he stammered.

I pushed the buzzer for Odette to return. When the door eased open again less than five seconds later, I assumed she'd been close by. I was horrified when I saw the last person in the world I ever expected to see again: Homer.

My breath caught in my throat and my stomach churned. "What are you doing here?" I asked with my lips quivering.

With a wild-eyed look on his face, Homer swaggered over to the bed, totally ignoring Ronald. "My Lord, Vanessa! I just found out this morning from Madeline what you've been up to all these months! How come you didn't tell me any of this?" He paused and stared at Ronald with a curious look on his face. "May I ask who you are, bro?"

"He's the recipient," I blurted out.

"Ronald Guthrie," Ronald added, extending his hand. I was glad his voice sounded strong again. Homer hesitated before he shook hands. "And you are?"

"Me? I'm Homer Lilly. Vanessa and I have been acquainted for years. Had I known what she's been going through since November, I would have come around more." Homer snorted and looked at me with his eyes narrowed. "I don't know why you thought you couldn't tell me about this."

It took a lot to make me angry. I avoided tense situations as much as I could because I didn't like confrontations. But Homer's presence and behavior had me reeling so hard, I was close to losing my composure. "That e-mail you sent me after our last date gave me the impression that you didn't want to be bothered," I said stiffly.

He threw his hands up. "Hold on now. That wasn't the case, Vanessa. You took that out of context. Maybe I was a little too hasty, but I still thought we'd remain friends," Homer said defensively. He reared back on his legs and placed his hands on his hips.

"Is that why you blocked me from responding to your e-mail?"

"You have my phone number and address. If you'd really wanted to communicate with me, you could have. When you didn't, what else could I presume and—"

I was elated when Odette entered the room before he could finish his last sentence. She briefly acknowledged Homer, apologized for interrupting, and quickly wheeled Ronald back to his room. But Homer stayed.

Odette had left the door open, but Homer darted across the floor and closed it. He returned to my bedside with an exasperated look on his face. "Who is that dude to you, and how did you get mixed up with him?" he demanded with his arms folded and a stern look on his face. "When I tried to get the whole story from Madeline, she told me to talk to you."

"He's my friend. One of the closest friends I have these days," I said curtly.

"He must be *very* close for you to give him one of your kidneys."

I nodded. "You're right. He and I are very close." I

was on a roll, so I couldn't stop myself from adding, "I just met him last November and now that he's got a part of me in his body, we'll be close for life."

Homer shook his head. "I swear to God, I never thought you'd do something so drastic. I guess I don't know you as well as I thought." His voice and his face suddenly softened. "Um . . . listen, I still care about you, Vanessa, and I'm going to show you. I'll be checking up on you every day," he vowed. "I'm sorry about sending you that silly e-mail. If I hadn't drunk all that champagne that night, I wouldn't have done it. I don't know what I was thinking. I almost called you a few times. I was embarrassed to do it because of the way I'd jumped the gun and let you go. As soon as you're well enough, we'll start from scratch and see where we can go from there."

I appreciated Homer's attempt to make amends, but it was too late for us to be anything other than just friends. I didn't feel strong enough to tell him that at the moment, but I would do so in the very near future.

CHAPTER 22

Homer's unexpected visit had really caught me off guard. If I hadn't already been lying down, I would have fallen to the floor. Before I knew it, my stomach was in knots and sweat was sliding down my face. I was so glad the nurse's aide came to bathe me a few seconds after his last comment. If she hadn't, there was no telling how much longer he would have stayed.

By evening, I felt well enough to leave my room, and I didn't need a wheelchair. I couldn't move briskly like I normally did, so it was a slow, wobbly walk to Ronald's room. The door was ajar, so I pushed it open and entered. He was sitting up in bed watching TV. A smile immediately formed on his face when he saw me. "Hello, Vanessa. I was going to call you."

I stopped by the side of his bed. "I won't stay long.

I just wanted to come and apologize in person for what happened in my room earlier today."

"You don't have to apologize for anything." He snickered. "And just who is that dude? I don't remember you ever mentioning him."

"Pffftt." I rolled my eyes and shook my head. "He's one of my best friend's brothers-in-law. We tried to connect, but it didn't work."

"When you mentioned the 'last date' I got the impression that he was someone special to you. How long have you been dating him?"

"The date I mentioned was our first and last. By the time I got home, he had sent me an e-mail to tell me he didn't want to see me again because he thought I had negative energy."

Ronald looked like he wanted to laugh. "I got the boot from Jan the same way." We laughed at the same time. I didn't know about him, but when I did it, I felt a sharp twinge in my stomach. It lasted only a split second, so I didn't give it too much thought. I was eager to laugh some more.

"Believe it or not, the guy before Homer ended our relationship the same way." I laughed again. I didn't feel a twinge this time.

"You're kidding!"

"No, I'm not." I didn't laugh again, but Ronald did. When he stopped, I cleared my throat and said,

"Judith mentioned something about you ending things with Jan. . . ."

He nodded. "And I did it in person."

"Good for you. When I hear from Homer again, I'm going to tell him I don't think we should attempt to restore a relationship that never got off the ground in the first place," I said firmly.

I couldn't ignore the smug smile on Ronald's face. I smiled too.

We chatted a few more minutes before I hugged him and returned to my room.

I didn't know if Homer had unblocked me or not, so I didn't even consider e-mailing him. I had no desire to text him either. I hadn't checked, but he had probably blocked me from doing that, too. But I didn't want to wait for him to randomly show up at my place; I had to let him know before that happened. So, I had no choice but to call him up. He didn't answer his phone, and I refused to stoop low enough to "break up" with him in a voice mail, which I thought was even worse than an e-mail. I left him a message to call me back ASAP.

He called twenty minutes later. I didn't waste any time telling him what I had to say. He was surprised, but not as much as I was when he told me, "You don't know what a good man you're letting get away."

That was the last time Homer ever spoke to me.

* * *

I was released from the hospital the next afternoon. Judith drove me home and I was glad to be back in my own space. But within an hour, my apartment was swarming with folks, mostly the same ones who had visited me in the hospital. After only a couple of hours, I was so exhausted from all the attention, I asked Mama to discreetly encourage everybody to leave soon.

Within ten minutes, she and Daddy were the only ones in the house with me.

"Ronald really is a nice young man. I like him a lot," Mama said as she stood over my sink washing the collard greens she had insisted on cooking for my dinner.

"And he's got a lot going for him. He owns his own house and he's got a good job managing that high-end department store on Rhodes Avenue," Daddy tossed in. He and I occupied my kitchen table.

My mouth dropped open. "When did you two meet Ronald?"

"Yesterday. When we went to check on you and found out they had already released you—an hour before you told us they would—we decided to finally go meet this mystery man," Daddy answered.

"Debra and Gary went with us. They took a shine

to Ronald, too," Mama added. "He agreed to have dinner with us when he's able. He may be in our lives for a long time, and the more we know about him, the better we'll feel."

Ronald and I had called each other almost every day since his surgery two weeks ago. And several times, when Judith went to visit him at the hospital, I'd gone with her. I'd also gone a few times on my own.

I returned to work the first Monday in April and everything appeared to be back to normal. But the best part was, Ronald was doing better than Dr. Thomas had predicted. He was released the last day of the month and was scheduled to return to work in two weeks, but only if he felt up to it and with Dr. Thomas's approval. Ronald was the senior manager at Saxon's Department Store, a smaller, more upscale version of Walmart. He enjoyed his job as much as I enjoyed mine, so going back to work had done a lot for his morale. He was also making arrangements to move back into his house.

Judith invited me to go with her to see Ronald's place, and to see how he was doing on the first Saturday he'd been back home. I accepted without hesitation. His ranch-style, four-bedroom house didn't have a white-picket fence like I'd imagined. But it was idyllic anyway. Like Judith, he also had an impressive collection of African artifacts in his living room. There was a small park in the next block with a duck pond. It seemed like the perfect neighborhood for a kind and gentle man like Ronald. I could understand why he had chosen this to be the place where he wanted to raise the children he planned to have some day. The children he would never have had, had it not been for me. . . .

I was amazed at how good Ronald looked already. He had gained back the weight he'd lost, the dark shadows had disappeared from around his eyes, and his skin had a much healthier glow. The three of us chatted for only half an hour because Ronald had plans to meet up with some friends later that evening. I enjoyed the brief visit immensely. I hoped that I would get to visit again soon, but I didn't broach the subject that day. I was not about to put him on the spot and make him feel obligated to spend time with me when it was obvious he wanted to get on with his life.

Reverend Jackson called me up on a regular basis, and he occasionally visited me at home. I couldn't wait to be up and about again. Not only was I eager to return to church, I couldn't wait to go on three- to four-hour shopping sprees at my favorite malls, and to movies, the gym, and every other place I hadn't been to lately. In the meantime, I would communicate with people as often as I could by telephone, text, or e-mail.

Even with two toddlers and a busy social life, Debra still had time to call me almost every day. This evening, after assuring her that I was doing fine and didn't need her to come over and do anything for me, she asked the last thing I expected: "Has Ronald asked you for a date yet?"

I gasped so hard, it felt like I was about to swallow my tongue. "Date? Me and Ronald? What makes you think that man wants to take me out?"

"Girl, you can't be that dense. A blind man could see that he's in love with you."

Her last sentence almost stopped my heart. "You only saw him that one day at the hospital," I reminded. "How could you tell something like that?"

"I may be young, but I know love when I see it in somebody's eyes. Every time your name came up that day we visited him, he glowed like a firefly."

"Girl, please! What you saw in Ronald's eyes was relief and gratitude. I'm sure that if I'd donated a kidney to any other man, he'd be looking the same way. Romance is probably the last thing on his mind." Madeline was the only other person who had brought up this subject, during my coffee break with her and

Odette, the day after I'd met him. She hadn't mentioned it since. I wasn't ready to confess to Debra (or anyone else) that I had romantic feelings for Ronald. I hoped that if he felt the same way about me, he'd let me know soon, because I didn't know how much longer I could contain myself.

CHAPTER 23

When Ronald called me up the day after my conversation with Debra and asked if I wanted to join him and a few of his friends at his house for drinks this weekend, I thought she had gone behind my back and put him up to it. "It'll only be a handful of folks, but you're welcome to bring a date," he said.

He was doing well, but he had to go to Dr. Thomas's office for routine checkups twice a week for the next three months. Then twice a month for a year. After that, he only had to go every six months for the next three to five years—unless he developed post-recovery complications. Until then, it looked like he wanted to do as much socializing as possible.

I accepted the invitation. I wanted to see his lovely house—and him—again, but my "date" was Anna. The minute I introduced them, he made her feel so welcome, she took to him like a duck to water. I couldn't remember the last time I'd seen her so giddy.

As soon as she saw me standing alone after a brief chat with Ronald, she shot across the living-room floor and stopped in front of me. "Well?" she said with a smile forming on her lips.

I hunched my shoulders. "Well what?"

"What are you going to do now?" Anna dipped her head and gave me a knowing look. I gave her an eyeball roll and a dismissive wave, but she kept going in the same direction. "Ronald is so charming, and his sister seems like a really nice, down to earth person, too. So, what happens next?" She didn't give me time to answer. "He's available, you're available. Can you tell where I'm going with this?"

"Yes, to a dead end. You stop that! I've already been through this with my sister. Ronald and I are just friends, nothing more," I insisted.

A week after my visit to Ronald's house, I called him up to see how he was doing. He was busy packing for a weekend jaunt to Vegas with some friends to celebrate his thirty-first birthday. I was glad he was getting back into the swing of things and that we still kept in touch. However, I knew that there would come a time when we wouldn't communicate as often.

I still chatted or met up with Judith, but even my encounters with her had tapered off. When her husband came home for two weeks in May, she invited me to attend a party at her apartment so I could finally meet him. I went and had a good time, even though Ronald hadn't been able to make it. "He's in Nevada hiking with some friends, and next weekend they're flying down to Baja to do some fishing," Judith explained with a nostalgic look on her face. "I haven't seen him this happy since he got sick. Everyone is amazed that he's doing so well already. Dr. Thomas told Ronald before his surgery that it could take up to three or four months for him to fully recover. It's only been two and he's as fit as I am."

"I'm happy for him," I said with a sniff.

Except for Judith's neighbor, an elderly widower named Mr. Brock, I was the only person who had come to her party alone. I danced with him until his back went out. From that point on, Judith's barrel-chested, sharp-featured husband was the only man who paid any attention to me. Arthur was a good dancer and I enjoyed chatting with him. So, after Mr. Brock hobbled back to his apartment, I spent most of my time chatting with Arthur. I was having such a good time I didn't want to leave. But when everyone except me had left, I knew it was time for me to go home, too.

My life got a little more hectic toward the end of May. I went out with one of Gary's friends a few times, flew to Reno with Madeline and Odette to celebrate my thirty-third birthday, and the following weekend, I drove to Carmel with Mama and Daddy.

On the Saturday night of Memorial Day weekend, I went out with a guy I'd grown up with named Sammy Reed. He was getting married in a week. Gary had thrown a bachelor party for him at his apartment the night before, but I hadn't been able to attend because I'd had to go pick up Mama and Daddy in Oakland where they'd gone to visit some friends. On their way home, Daddy's car had broken down on the freeway and he had left his Triple A card at home, along with his wallet.

When Sammy and I approached the Spiderweb Club entrance with his arm around my shoulder, Ronald exited at the same time. He didn't look in my direction before he started walking briskly down the street. I was surprised to see that he was alone. Just as we were about to go inside, Ronald turned around and spotted me. After we waved to each other, he turned back around and started walking away even faster. "Who was that?" Sammy wanted to know.

"He's . . . just a friend," I said.

Ronald and I hadn't communicated since the previous week. Each time we talked, he updated me on the progress of his health. I didn't have any health issues for us to be concerned about, so the state of mine rarely came up. Other than the six-inch scar on my abdomen that Dr. Thomas assured me would fade over time, I had healed completely. He had also told me some donors could have long-term problems with

pain, nerve damage, hernias, and intestinal obstruc-
tion, but I wasn't going to mention that to anybody
unless it happened. The last thing I wanted to do was
give Ronald, or anybody, something else to worry
about.

Other than a few mundane questions about family
and work, he never asked about my personal life.
And I never asked him about his. However, Judith
had recently mentioned that he'd been seeing a new
woman. But the details had been so vague, I had no
idea if it was a serious relationship or not. It didn't
matter one way or the other to me anyway. As long as
he was happy and healthy, that was all I really cared
about.

CHAPTER 24

Things took a drastic turn for me in July. I'd spent the Fourth at Odette's backyard barbecue that evening. Mama and Daddy were visiting friends in Oakland, and everybody else I knew was busy. Instead of going home after the barbecue, I decided to go to a movie. *Jurassic World* had been released last month and was still playing at the mall a couple of miles from my apartment. The theater was so crowded, it took me a while to find somewhere to sit, which was a middle seat five rows from the screen. I sat down, but before I could get comfortable, the man on my left tapped my arm. "Hello, Vanessa." It was Ronald.

"H-hi," I stammered, glancing to his other side. I was so flustered, I spilled popcorn in his lap. "I'm surprised to see you here," I went on as I brushed off his lap.

He chuckled. "Going to the movies is one of my favorite pastimes."

"Mine too," I said in a meek tone. I didn't know how much longer I could keep my feelings about him to myself. I didn't know who to tell first. But it wouldn't be Ronald! I had no idea what was going on in his love life, and I still couldn't bring myself to make the first move. If I did and he rejected me, I'd feel like a fool.

"I spent most of the day at Judith's place. After all the barbecue was gone, she and a couple of her friends decided to drive down to Vegas. There was no place else I wanted to go, so here I am."

I wondered what had happened to the woman Judith told me he'd been dating. . . .

"I attended a get-together at Odette's house. But after that ended, I wasn't ready to go home. So, here I am, too."

Ronald glanced around the semidarkened room. "Are you here with somebody?" he asked.

"Um . . . no. I'm here alone," I said shyly.

He snorted and leaned closer. "I saw you and your date going into the Spiderweb a few weeks ago. I would have stopped and said something to you, but I didn't want to cause you any problems with him. . . ."

I was flattered. I could tell when a man was fishing for more information that might benefit him. I couldn't reveal it fast enough. I snickered before I said, "That wasn't a real date.'" Ronald looked relieved when I explained my relationship to Sammy. I had never felt so awkward in my life. Not only was I in the company of one of the most charming and handsome single men I knew, he had one of my kidneys!

Somewhere along the way, I had recently developed a strange mental connection to Ronald. At least once or twice a week, I'd suddenly find myself wondering what he was doing and with whom. I also wondered if he was living a healthy lifestyle and not doing anything to jeopardize *my* kidney. I had to keep reminding myself that it was *his* kidney now. But no matter where he went, there would literally always be part of me with him. I didn't like to think about our physical "connection" in those terms too often. Because when I did, I actually got light-headed. I lowered my voice to a whisper: "People are giving us mean looks, so we'd better be quiet."

"Let's move to the back row then," he suggested. Before I knew it, he had my hand and was leading me away.

"This is better," Ronald said when we plopped down in two end seats in the last row. "And more comfortable."

"Yes, it is," I agreed. We didn't speak again until the movie ended. I stood up first. "Well, it was nice to see you tonight. I'll be in touch with you again soon."

"Wait! Can I buy you a drink?"

"I'm sorry. I drink alcohol only on special occasions," I said with a shy grin.

"So, this is a special occasion to me."

I was glad there was a bar in the next block so we could walk. Not less than five minutes after we'd slid into a booth and ordered a beer for him and a club soda for me, he hauled off and kissed me.

CHAPTER 25

It had been so long since I'd been kissed, I had almost forgotten what it felt like. It felt good.

When Ronald pulled away from me, I was so stunned, a flea could have knocked me over. "That was nice," I managed. I exhaled and slid my tongue across my bottom lip. I couldn't remember the last time my heart had thumped so hard. I had on a loose blouse, so it looked like I was just smoothing wrinkles on it when I rubbed my chest.

"I've been wanting to do that for a long time," he confessed.

I gave him an incredulous look. "What? But . . ." My voice suddenly sounded so hoarse, I thought I had developed an acute case of laryngitis.

"Vanessa, we don't need to beat around the bush. You know as well as I do that this was a long time coming."

I hunched my shoulders. "I never thought about

it." I was too embarrassed to come clean and admit that I'd been thinking the same thing myself.

Ronald looked embarrassed too. He started tapping the top of the table with his fingers and fidgeting in his seat. "If I'm out of line, I apologize. And if you never want to speak to me again after tonight, I'll understand."

"It's okay. Uh . . . if you thought this was a 'long time coming,' how come you never asked me out?"

"I wanted to. But you're one of the busiest and most popular women I know."

I giggled. "Yeah, right. I'm so busy and popular that I'm at the movies on a Saturday night on my own, on the Fourth of July at that." We laughed.

"The same thing goes for me," he said. We laughed again.

Ronald followed me to my apartment in his shiny new Volvo. We spent the next few hours on my living-room couch getting to know each other a little better. I was amazed that after all this time, I was just finding out that we liked some of the same movies, books, and food. After chatting for another hour, I was convinced that he had everything I wanted in a man.

It was daylight when I walked him to the door. "So, where do we go from here?" I asked. "We shouldn't move too fast, though."

He reared back and bucked his eyes in mock horror. "Too fast? We've known each other for eight months. At the rate we're going, we'll spend our first real date as residents at that retirement home where your folks live." We laughed long and loud.

"When did you know . . . ?" I couldn't finish my sentence.

"That I was in love with you?" He shrugged his shoulders. "I can't really say for sure. The first day I laid eyes on you, I felt something." When he kissed me this time, I didn't want him to stop. But a few seconds later when he did, he caressed the side of my face and looked into my eyes. "Why don't you think things through for a few days? When you feel like talking, give me a call or come to my house." He left right after he said that.

I hadn't been to sleep since the day before, but I didn't even bother going to bed. I was so hyped up, I knew I'd never be able to sleep. I had to decide whom I was going to share the news about Ronald and me with first. When Madeline called me up at nine a.m. Sunday morning to see if I was going to meet her and Odette for coffee after church, I figured I'd start with her. The whole time I was telling her about my night out with Ronald, she remained as silent as a mouse. When I finally stopped talking, she asked, "When's the wedding?"

"Oh hush! We didn't get anywhere near something that serious. For now, we're going to spend time together and see what happens."

After I'd spoken to everybody else close to me and listened to them whoop and holler their approval, I dialed Judith's number. I decided to call her last because I assumed Ronald wanted to be the one to tell her about us first. She interrupted me right after I told her that he and I were convinced that we'd be good for each other. "He told me the same thing. But do you really love him?" She sounded so somber and distant, I didn't know what to think.

"Yes, I guess I do," I said in a shaky tone.

"You 'guess' you do? Vanessa, love is not something you guess at. Either you do or you don't. I thought Jan loved my brother and he thought the same thing. I know he's where he's at now because of you, but I don't want you to be with him out of pity—"

I couldn't interrupt her fast enough. "Hold on now. I never said anything about pitying Ronald. I care about him the way I've always wanted to care about a man. But I will admit that if he hadn't initiated things, I probably never would have."

"From what he's told me, I have a feeling he cares more about you than you care about him."

"Judith, there is probably not a relationship in the world between a man and a woman where the love is equally balanced. For all you and I know, I may care more about him than he cares about me."

"I just don't want to see him get hurt again."

I was disappointed and surprised that Judith was so apprehensive. But after all she'd been through with him, I understood where she was coming from. "At the end of the day, Ronald is a grown man and you can't protect him for the rest of his life." I immediately wished I could take my words back. Judith gasped so loudly, she whimpered. "Oh! I didn't mean that the way it sounded."

"I'm sure you didn't," she mumbled. "Well, I wish you and Ronald all the luck in the world. If things don't work out, I hope we'll still be friends. I don't know what I would have done without you."

By September, I knew I wanted to be with only Ronald for the rest of my life. All I needed was for him to propose. However, he must have been on a different page because by November, he hadn't brought up the subject of marriage one single time.

Sunday was November 22, the anniversary of the day Ronald and I had first met. When I brought it to his attention, his eyes lit up like a lightning bug. "And I haven't forgotten about that promise I made to foot the bill for your long-overdue trip to Paris. The one you missed out on because of me." We had just come from dinner and were sitting on my living-room couch that night.

"The one I missed out on because the post office sent my passport to the wrong address."

Ronald shook his head. "No, they didn't. It landed right where it was supposed to." I blinked to hold back my tears and racked my brain to come up with what to say next. Before I could say another word, he added, "All you need to do is let me know when you want to take that trip."

"Well, it's too late for me to go this year for Christmas. Maybe I'll go next year. Mama said she'd like to see Paris at least one more time, so maybe she'll go with me."

"It's never too late to book a trip if you're traveling first class. I'm sure you and your mom would have a lot of fun, but do you really want to spend such a romantic time of year in Paris with Mama? Not only will you be surrounded by newlyweds, there will be hundreds of other couples there, too. All celebrating their love for each other."

I punched the side of his arm. "Well, if you feel that way, why don't you go with me?" I teased.

"That's fine. I've never traveled with a married woman. . . ."

My breath caught in my throat. I sucked in so much air I thought I was going to pop wide open. "W-what in the world—?"

Ronald cut me off by covering my mouth with his hand. "Will you marry me?"

I pushed his hand away from my face and said, "Yes."

He wanted to get married the week of Christmas, so we didn't have enough time to plan a big church wedding. I had given up on that a long time ago anyway. Nobody questioned the fact that we didn't want to put it off too long. And nobody admitted it, but I was certain that they had the same concern I had: the future of Ronald's health. All of his follow-up appointments had gone well so far, but he still had a long way to go before he was completely out of the woods.

CHAPTER 26

The next couple of weeks were chaotic. I had Facebook, Twitter, and Instagram accounts, but I hadn't posted anything about myself and Ronald yet. I had always been a very private person, so I didn't broadcast every little detail of my personal life on social media the way some folks did. But it seemed like every friend, relative, and coworker Ronald and I had immediately shared our story on social media when we announced our engagement.

Debra was over the moon. Two weeks before the wedding, I had lunch with her at Juanita's. As much as she liked Mexican food, she ignored her super tacos and stared at me with a pensive look on her face for almost half a minute after we'd sat down. "You'd better start eating before your food gets cold," I told her. I had already started devouring my burrito.

She tilted her head to the side and let out a loud

sigh. "I'm so happy for you, V. I'm glad something exciting finally happened in our lives. You and Ronald are Internet celebrities."

I chuckled. "I don't feel like one. I still do the same things now that I did before all this started."

Debra rolled her eyes. "You are big news, girl! People are going to be talking about you for a long time, so you'd better get used to it."

"My fifteen minutes of fame can't last too much longer," I countered. "People will probably forget about me by next month and move on to somebody more interesting."

"Stop trying to be so modest." Debra paused long enough to catch her breath and then she started up again, speaking louder and faster. She hadn't touched her tacos yet. "Most of my recent Facebook posts are about you and Ronald. I want all of my social media friends to know what an awesome big sister I have. When you have time, I'd like to show you some of the comments I've received. People who don't even know you are almost as excited as I am." Debra finally picked up one of her tacos, but she still didn't eat. "By the way, Stephen is going to get in touch with you. He wants to write something about you and Ronald."

I gulped. "For the newspaper?"

"Of course! And for my sake, I hope you let him."

Some of the pieces my brother-in-law wrote for our city newspaper were often featured on the front page. His editor received tons of positive feedback on a regular basis from readers about some of them. Therefore, I was not surprised to hear that Stephen wanted to do a human interest story about Ronald and me.

Two days after my lunch with Debra, he called me up. By now I was ready to share my story with the world. Stephen wanted to come over right away but it had been such an exhausting day at the office, all I wanted to do was kick back in front of my TV. I agreed to meet with him the next evening. "Okay, V. And if it's okay with you, I'd like for Ronald to be present so I can get his input firsthand. Most of the people who read my articles are women and they are always interested in a man's point of view."

"I would like for him to be present too. After all, this is not just about me. I'll give him a call right away," I replied. We ended our conversation and I immediately dialed Ronald's number. I got his voice mail so I left a message for him to call me back at his earliest convenience, but I didn't tell him why.

He returned my call ten minutes later. "I'm sorry I didn't answer when you called. I was taking a shower. What's up?"

"How do you feel about being the subject of a newspaper article?" I asked.

"Me?" He laughed.

"Actually, both of us. My brother-in-law wants to do a piece and publish it in the Lifestyle section. That's where they feature the uplifting and inspirational stories. The last one he wrote was about a two-year-old collie named Boscoe that had become so unruly, his elderly owner decided to give him to his teenage grandsons. The day before the boys came to get the dog, a fire broke out in the man's apartment while he was taking his daily afternoon nap. If Boscoe hadn't jumped into his bed and licked his face until he woke up, he would have died."

"I read about that! The old gentleman decided to keep the dog after all!" Ronald exclaimed. He suddenly sounded downright giddy. "When does Stephen want to get together?"

"Can you come over around seven tomorrow evening?"

"I'll be there with bells on." We laughed.

Stephen joined us at my apartment the next day and we gave him all the information he needed. He wrote the article the same night. It was published in the following Sunday edition. Three days later, Stephen's editor called Ronald and me to let us know how many calls, e-mails, and letters the newspaper had already received, praising them for doing the piece.

Before we knew it, hundreds of people who'd read about us took to the Internet and our story went viral. Ronald and I were bombarded with messages and comments, all positive. I was stunned when I received an e-mail from Barry. He didn't even mention the last one he'd sent me. All he said was that he **wished me well**, and that he was **sorry things didn't work out between us.** I never expected to hear from Homer again, so I was shocked when he sent me another e-mail, too. All this one said was: **Congratulations and good luck.**

Ronald and I responded to some of the messages, but with all the other things going on in our lives, we didn't have time to reply to them all.

But there was one that really stood out. It was from a woman in Liverpool, England. She had recently been approved to donate one of her kidneys to her fiancé, but had backed out a week before the surgery. When she read about us, she immediately changed her mind. They were married in the hospital chapel the day after the transplant. Their story went viral on social media more quickly than ours. What was so fascinating to everybody was the fact that this had started because my passport had been sent to the wrong address.

Debra was really getting a big kick out of everything. Each day she had something new up her sleeve.

Somehow she had managed to get photos someone had taken of me and Ronald in the recovery room after the surgery. "I'm going to post these on Facebook, so long as you don't mind," she told me.

"Even if I did mind, you'd badger me until I gave in," I teased. "Go ahead and post them. They are unflattering and I hope the people who don't know me don't think I look that haggard."

"Girl, after what you did for Ronald; even if you looked like Godzilla, nobody would call you haggard."

By the end of the following week, a lot of the pandemonium had fizzled out. Ronald and I got to spend time together alone almost every single day at my apartment, or his house.

It was still an exhausting time for me, but I was more concerned about how all this hectic activity was impacting Ronald's recovery. He still had to take medications, but he appeared to be as physically fit as I was. However, I couldn't wait for things to die down completely so we could move forward and enjoy normal lives. Besides, if my time with Ronald was going to be limited, I didn't want to waste one single day trying to avoid the people who were still hounding us with the same questions and comments.

I never mentioned to anyone my concern that Ronald might only live a few more years, mainly because I had no reason to think that he wouldn't live a long and healthy life. One of the things that gave me hope was the fact that Mama had had her transplant surgery almost forty years ago, and she'd never had any problems.

Ronald and I were married on December 20 (the same day I was supposed to go to Paris last year), in his living room in the presence of forty of our friends, relatives, and coworkers. He wore a black tuxedo and I wore the beautiful white gown Mama had worn on her big day. Right after Reverend Jackson pronounced us man and wife, Daddy moved closer and whispered in my ear, "Baby, next to your mama, you are the most beautiful bride I've ever seen. I'm so blessed to have such an amazing daughter. Ronald hit the jackpot."

"So did I," I said proudly.

Stephen's editor had even come with a photographer who was going to take pictures to go with the follow-up piece Stephen was writing about us.

There was a huge, beautifully decorated Christmas tree in Ronald's living room. Not only were there numerous gifts underneath it, there were just as many wedding gifts. The large sheet cake Debra had baked had been devoured immediately, and so had most of the snacks she'd had a caterer deliver. This was the first time any of our guests had celebrated Christmas and a wedding at the same time.

Ronald and I were scheduled to leave for our honeymoon immediately after our wedding reception. We had already packed. The first thing I'd put in my suitcase was my passport, the catalyst that had started it all. I planned to have it framed someday.

My wedding day was the most important day of my life, but it was Anna's two-month-old son, Aaron, who received most of the attention. And I didn't mind at all. I had received enough in the last few months to last me a lifetime.

"Okay now, V, when can we expect you to bless us with a new grandchild?" Daddy asked, speaking so loudly everybody in the living room got quiet and immediately looked at me.

I didn't need to be a mind reader to know that some of the guests had been avoiding that subject. "Soon, I hope," I blurted out. Ronald and I had already discussed becoming parents. We loved children and wanted to start our family as soon as possible. I couldn't ignore the possibility that he wouldn't live long enough to see our children grow up, though. I'd been thinking about it ever since he asked me to marry him, especially today.

I had dismissed that grim thought by the time the reception ended, but on the flight to Paris, it returned. It didn't stay long, though.

The moment I laid eyes on Paris, I felt the magic Mama had told me about. I hadn't felt as vibrant, hopeful, and energetic since I was a teenager. Before we got comfortable in our hotel penthouse, with a fabulous view of the Eiffel Tower, I felt like a new and better person. It no longer mattered to me if Ronald and I had only a short time together. My future was still as bright as the City of Lights.

EPILOGUE

December 2019

So many wonderful things had happened in the last four years. Anna had two children now and was pregnant with her third. My footloose brother had married his girlfriend last year and they'd recently purchased a beautiful house. Mama and Daddy had a few new minor health issues, but they were still as active as ever. Debra had kept her promise to them and resumed her education now that her children were in school full time.

When I resigned from the job I'd loved so much, six months after my wedding, Jim actually cried. He called me at home so often, you would have thought I was still on the payroll. Sometimes he called just to reminisce about past work-related social events. And then there were the times when he admitted that he'd only called to hear my voice. I had lunch with him at least once a month, but he still called me up, too.

Dennis remarried last year and moved to Montana, but we still kept in touch. Judith's husband finally ended his long career with the military two years ago. Her son had graduated and landed a great job in DC. Judith was as giddy as a teenager now. I knew that one of the reasons was that she was no longer responsible for Ronald's care.

Both of Madeline's children were honor roll students. Odette's two daughters were studying at UC Berkeley, and her eldest had recently become engaged. Despite our lives being busier than ever, we still found time to get together.

We were celebrating our fourth wedding anniversary today. Ronald had insisted on doing it in Paris, in the same luxurious penthouse hotel suite where we'd spent our honeymoon. Debra had offered to take care of our children, three-year-old Ronald Jr. and two-year-old Patricia.

"Mama, where is Paris?" Junior asked. He and his sister were standing in the middle of our bedroom floor watching Ronald and me pack. We were going to drop them off at Debra's house on our way to the San Jose airport, which was about forty-five minutes away.

"It's a beautiful city in France, sweetie," I replied.

"Where is France?" Junior asked next with a con-

fused look on his face. He had my skin-tone and facial features and Patricia was the spitting image of
Ronald.

"It's a country in Europe," Ronald answered as he
closed his suitcase and glanced around the room. "I
hope I'm not forgetting anything," he mumbled.

Junior looked even more confused. "Where is Europe?"

"Honey, it's too complicated to go into now. We'll
take you there some day," I said.

Patricia's vocabulary was still very limited so she
didn't speak in complete sentences yet. Ronald and I
gasped when she asked, "I go to Paris too?"

"Yes, you'll 'go to Paris too,' baby," Ronald told
her.

I was glad when we finally boarded our early morning flight, which would last almost sixteen hours.
Ronald slept most of the way. I slept in snatches every
hour or so and read several magazines from cover to
cover. It was a comfortable journey, but I was glad
when our plane finally landed.

We hadn't been back to Paris since our honeymoon, so I was anxious to get out and about and see
how much it had changed. We were a little tired, but
right after we unpacked, we bolted from our room.
We revisited a couple of our favorite spots and took
dozens of pictures along the way. After visiting the
Eiffel Tower and snapping more pictures, we decided

to eat dinner at a new restaurant that had been a nightclub the last time we visited. We stuffed ourselves with lamb, caviar, grilled veggies, thick slices of French bread, and some of the best wine I'd ever tasted.

I was having so much fun, I could barely contain myself.

When we got back to our hotel, we were so exhausted, we fell asleep as soon as our heads hit the pillows.

Despite the awesome time I was having, the city didn't have the same magic as the first time. It didn't matter because I'd received all the magic I needed.

DISCUSSION QUESTIONS

1. Would you ever consider donating an organ to a stranger?

2. Would you donate an organ to someone you knew?

3. Did Vanessa decide too quickly to become an organ donor?

4. Did you predict that Vanessa and Ronald would fall in love after she gave him one of her kidneys?

5. Some transplant recipients live only a few years after their surgery. Do you think they should not have children because they might not be around to raise them?

6. What do you think about people who end relationships by e-mail, text, or some other impersonal way? Has it ever happened to you? If so, how did you feel?

7. Do you believe that everything happens for a reason?

8. If you believe in fate, do you think it played a role in bringing Ronald and Vanessa together by sending her passport to the wrong address?

9. Ronald's health issues and uncertain future overwhelmed his fiancée, Jan, so she broke off their engagement. She regretted it and resumed her relationship with him. However, he eventually ended their engagement himself. Did you think he'd be better off without her?

10. If you were in love with someone who developed serious health issues, would you stay in the relationship?

11. Vanessa was reluctant to share her story with the world, but she eventually did. If you were in a similar situation, would you want to remain anonymous and protect your privacy?

12. Vanessa had never had much luck with men. She hit the jackpot with Ronald. Do you think she was such a prize, he hit the jackpot, too?

13. Did you think Vanessa would ever get to spend a Christmas in Paris?

Don't miss any of
Mary Monroe's
heartwarming holiday novellas
REMEMBRANCE
RIGHT BESIDE YOU
and
THE GIFT OF FAMILY
Available now from Dafina Books
Wherever books are sold